The Adventures of Sky Hawkins and Duane McSwaine

the Mysterious Diary

The Curtis C-46 Commando in flight.

Mark Barra

Fulton Books, Inc.
Meadville, PA

Published by Fulton Books 2021

ISBN 978-1-64654-033-4 (paperback)
ISBN 978-1-64654-034-1 (digital)

Printed in the United States of America

I dedicate this book to my parents, Joseph and Mary Barra, for they worked hard to give me a good home. They grew up during the Depression. My Dad told stories about it, when he served in the CCCamps in the 40s and my Mom told stories when she was a little girl. I miss very much. I decided to write about their times in the '20s and '30s and '40s and I started writing this when I was 34 I am 62 now and I decided to finish it and share with you the readers about their times and make it into an adventure book for the whole family to enjoyed.

I also want to thank my daughter, Gina Marie Barra, for she's my inspiration in my life. She misses her grandma and never got to meet her grandpa.

Also I want to thank all those who serve in the Armed Forces (If it wasn't for their bravery and Sacrifice this book won't be possible they gave their lives so others may live free!)

Contents

Introduction

In 1936, there were special squadrons assembled together, they were attached to flying Tigers,23rd fighting group the sacrifice made before the second world war layed ground for the Japanese defeat! Here a squad of brave men (fictional) On the president's request, from the Army air corp and the Marine corps and Navy pilots 3 squadrons (the first American Volunteer Group) Republic of China Air Force (AVG) called themselves the "SkyHawks." They went through special basic training. They knew everything from demolition to martial arts.

When they went on their secret missions for the president, only 3 out of 7 came back. Their names were Nick Washburn, Duane McSwaine and Sky Hawkins. They became the best of friends in remembrance of their fallen comrades in the Red China Sea who battled against the Japanese Zeros.

Here are the wild adventures of Sky Hawkins and Duane Elton McSwaine.

The Mysterious Diary

It was a stormy rainy afternoon. 14 year old James Michael Stern III was babysitting 3 sisters as their parents went out to James sr. business lunch date with his clients from work, Patty oldest 12 and his two youngest are 10, Kelly Ann and Gina Marie Stern. They were twins and Patty was playing her records and Kelly talking on the phone Gina playing with her Maine Coon black kitty, she just got for her birthday she named her Missy that James gave her because he knows how much Gina loves cats.

James checked up on them to see if they were all right. "By the sound of it, they were," he said to himself, laughing as he listened in on them.

Then he decided to go up to the attic to look around for his baseball cleats and left-handed glove. He came across a trunk he never noticed before. "It must be Grandma's old trunk that Dad brought up here last weekend," James said, and so he decided to open it up to see what was inside. "I'm so curious what Grandma was saving after all these years." James unlocked the latch in the middle of the trunk, and as he opened it, he found uniforms on top and an old diary of brown leather with a brass lock.

"Hey, it's the mysterious diary that Dad always talked about!" James said to himself.

He looked deeper into the trunk and found the key that opened the diary. He put on his grandfather's leather jacket and his officer's cap and sat right in front of the chest with his back leaning against the trunk and opened up the dairy. He was amazed to find a drawing identical to a painting in his dad's den.

It was his grandfather and his best friend, Duane Elton McSwaine, when they had served together during the French Indochina War and World War II.

James stared at the picture with goosebumps running up and down his arms and said, "Here is someone I would have loved to spend time with. If he was still alive." Then tears came falling from his face as he started turning the pages and started reading the diary. And that's where our story begins.

CHAPTER 1

Born in the Ghetto

It was a cold windy day in the Southside of Chicago, in the Cook County Hospital, where a boy was born. James Michael Stern came into the world weighing ten pounds and was nine inches tall.

James Michael Stern was born October 9, 1914, and his proud parents were Ralph and Julia Stern.

Strong Catholic background, his Dad was Irish and his Mom was Italian descent They lived in the Southside near Comiskey Park, (Home of the Chicago White Sox) block away, in a three-family house on 371 South Main Street.(James loved baseball and went to every game he could)he played stick ball with Neighborhood kids! and his cousin Jack Stern used to come from Hyde Park play stick ball with James and Vinny he was His favorite cousin on his Dad's side of the family.

Backyard was cement, and underneath their pouch, trash cans were infested with rats. Over the fence was a train yard, where steam engines were blowing steam and making their way into the yard, whistle-blowing, freight being loaded and unloaded in the freight yard.

It was a poor neighborhood. James grew up learning how to fight in the streets. He had to learn quickly to adapt and defend himself against rival gangs in the late '20s and early '30s. He got to know the streets real well and learned how to survive the rough neighborhood of Southside. He got to know respect by Black children in the neighborhood. He became good friends with one of them in particular; his name was Vinny Leroy Jones, one of the toughest kids in the neighborhood.

James and Vinny and cousin Jack (Jimmy nicknamed Jack scooter)hung together a lot. Vinny looked out for Jack and James; there were skinny kids at the time, but tough to put down in the streets, The fighting Irish and Italian in Them made Them mean and tough on the streets of Chicago.

They played pool together, basketball, baseball and rode motorbikes, even stole Jimmy Dads red pick up truck when they were 13 Jimmy loves adventures, getting in trouble with Jack and Vinny they also double-dating taking their girlfriends to hyde park to Jack house drinking Uncle Andy's beer and played poker at their tree house stealing beer and cigarettes and when they needed money they hussle making money by taking passengers bags from and to the train station for 50 cents a day and they even learned how to use a .45 at the age of thirteen. They had grown up quick and street smart to survive. One night around the evening, James, Jack and Vinny were coming home from the neighborhood clubhouse they belonged to when they heard a scream so terrifying, they both looked at each other and wondered.

"What was that?" asked James.

But Jack was curious and wanted to see what happened, so the boys went around a dark alley, and at the back of the clubhouse was a woman being raped by four thugs. James grabbed one of boys off the woman and punched him hard in the face, and Jack, Vinny grabbed the other two off her and punched them in the stomach, and the other one ran off as the 3 boys helped the poor woman up on her feet, and James wrapped his leather jacket around her and wiped her tears from her face. As she was limping out of the alley, James and Jack carried her as Vinny looked out for any more trouble as they carried her out of the dark alley.

Vinny asked, "Where are you taking her to?"

James said quietly, "To my house. Mom would know what to do!"

As they made their way to James's apartment to carry the beat-up and bruised woman upstairs; they opened the door and put the woman on the couch.

James yelled out, "Hey, Mom, come quick, I have a hurt woman in the parlor, please help me." James cried out to his mom, who just finished the dishes.

She came into the room and said, "James, what have you boys done?" Thinking her son hurt her bad.

But James said, "Mom, it was thugs that did this to her."

She went into the bathroom, got a pan of water and a face cloth and wiped the poor woman's face.

Jimmy and Vinny, Jack looked at each other in amazement at how a woman of her weight and size was still alive.

Vinny said, "Hey, Jimmy, I must go. I'll catch you tomorrow at school, okay?"

Jimmy replied, "Okay, I'll see you at school."

He went out the door and into the street as James looked on, seeing his mom cleaning the poor woman up and found a new dress for her to wear.

And the woman said, "Thank you for all you have done for me, my name is Shawna Baker. I'm very grateful for your son and his Cousin and Friend helping me." Jack told Aunt Julie he must go home now hugged her and shook James hand waved goodbye and out the door he went.

Mrs. Stern asked the woman if she would like to stay the night and rest, "James will walk you home on his way to school."

She smiled and nodded her head and fell fast asleep on the couch as Julia put a blanket over her and said to James, "What a shame this had happened."

It was a chilly Monday morning, about five, when Ralph woke up and walked out into the parlor and saw this Black skinny woman on his couch, wrapped up in a blanket, and he stared at her for a moment and went into the kitchen to make some breakfast.

Julia heard rattling in the kitchen, so she got up and took a glance at the woman still sleeping and went into the kitchen, and Ralph asked, "Who is that woman, and why is she here?"

Julia explained, "James, Jack and Vinny found her in the alley last night being raped by some thugs."

Ralph looked up. "Julia, how bad is she, does she need to go to the hospital?"

Julia replied, "No, just minor cuts and bruises. James will walk her home when he goes to school this morning."

"Oh, okay, just make sure she is safe going home, okay? I need to leave early to go to work in the freight yard, I got some delivery to make. I'll be home late. All the stops I have to make. The train came in late last night, so I left early, got home straight to bed because I know it's going to be a busy day today."

Monday morning clouds were rolling in, and the wind was picking up as the cold air blew as Ralph made his way to the streets. As he was walking along in the alley to the freight yard, it started to snow heavily as the wind blew like needles into the face. Snow started to get heavy onto his feet as he made his way to the freight yard, covering his face with his collar and holding on to his hat. He finally made it to the train depot, shaking snow off his jacket and hat.

James was woken up by his mother pulling blankets off him. "Time to go to school," she said. "Get dressed and eat your breakfast, Jimmy."

Jimmy was rubbing his eyes and coughed. "Mom, I don't feel good today, may I stay home and rest?" he asked.

"No, Jimmy," she answered. "You remember the young woman you brought home last night? You must walk her home, her family must be worried."

James stared at his mom. "What woman? I must have fallen fast asleep and forgot about her."

"Jimmy, she's sleeping on the couch," she replied. "Now get dressed and come into the kitchen."

So Jimmy got dressed and went into the kitchen as the woman woke up and followed James into the kitchen. They both sat down and ate as Julia looked up upon them and said, "Hurry up, going to be late. I must meet Janice at the bus stop at eight, get my hair done, and buy a cake for dad's birthday tomorrow. I want to surprise him."

"Boy, a cake for Dad, WOW!," James replied. "I can't wait, Mom, catch you later," James said on his way out with Shawna as they shut the door and went out into the snowstorm! "Boy, Shawna, it is very bad out here, I'm wondering how much snow we are getting."

Shawna replied to a lot of snow by the looks of run and slide all the way to where she lives five blocks away on the third floor of an apartment building. They said their goodbyes, and that was the last time; they never met again because of how the neighborhood was tough and cruel. She smiled and waved goodbye.

James made it to Southside Middle School on Old Waterbury Hill Road at 7:45 AM. He went in to warm up and made it in before the first bell.

Meanwhile, Julia was getting ready to meet Janice at the bus stop. She got her coat and hat and was out the door. She went and locked the door behind her as she went down the stairs and opened the outside door and down to short cement stairs and into the street. She started to walk with her head down and scarf wrapped around her face. As she stepped off the curb, a car struck her, and she went over the hood and into the snowy road. The car couldn't stop because of ice and snow and the oncoming car from the other direction and it ran her over.

She was dead at the age of thirty, just cut down at her prime. She didn't see it coming; it happened so fast, both drivers couldn't stop in time to save her. A crowd of people gathered, looking out their window from the sidewalk, all gazing at a lifeless woman whom James adored hopelessly.

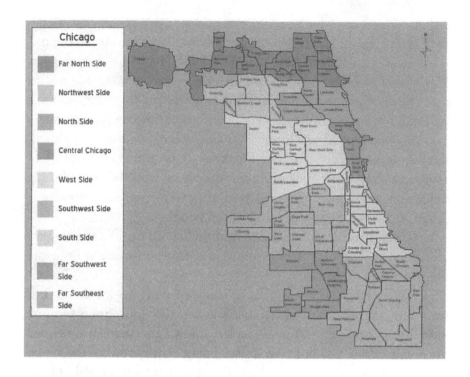

Police arrived late, and the ambulance too; snow almost covered her lifeless body by the time they arrived and brought her to the morgue, looking for her address, something to identify her. She only had her family picture in her purse, a key, a rosary, a hanky, and the fifty dollars to buy her husband a cake.

Police recognized the boy from fights and from hanging at a pool hall. "Hey," one cop said. "That is the kid from the pool hall, picked him up for fighting at Rack and Play pool hall on Green Street a couple of weeks ago."

One officer replied, "Oh yeah, that's right."

The other officer said, "Where does he go to school?"

"Oh yeah, Southside Middle School on Old Waterbury Hill Road," one officer said.

Then the other officer said, "That's right, let's go tell him the bad news."

They went to Southside Middle School on Old Waterbury Hill Road. As they approached the school and looked up at the window on the second floor, there was James looking down at them, wondering what was going on and saying to himself, "Are they going to arrest me? Good, I want to get out of here it's boring here, teacher's assignment dragging me down, I'd rather be home eating my dad's birthday cake anyhow when mom brings it home tonight. I can't wait." He said this to himself as police entered the building.

The head principal came into the room with the police officer behind her. Mrs. Brown asked, "Can I see James, please?"

James heard and stood up good. He yelled out, "I want to get out of the boring class anyway," as he walked up to the principal and said, "Hi, Mrs. Anderson, I'm here ready to go home."

Mrs. Anderson looked at James and sighed, saying, "These policemen have something to tell you."

One officer said, "Son, let's step outside." While other classmates looked puzzled and watched as police put their hand on his shoulder as they were walking out the classroom door.

James looked up at the officers and said, "I didn't do anything wrong today. I was here all along."

Both police officers sat poor James on the hallway bench and told him as carefully as possible that his mom was killed crossing the street this morning by passing cars.

James was dumbfounded. "Nooooo!" he cried out. "This is not true!" he yelled loudly as the class heard him through the door.

"Son, I'm sorry," one officer said. "It's true, we have her in the morgue right now."

"Nooooo!" cried out James. "Stop lying to me, stop. I hate you both for telling me this. I want to see her now!" He cried out as police walked James to the police car and to the hospital where she was.

James went to see his mom for the very last time and cried, saying, "My sweet mother, why in God's name you left me when I need you the most." And he fell to the floor, sobbing as his father just arrived to see her laying on a gurney and his son lying next to her sobbing on her lifeless body. Ralph put his arms around his son and kissed his beloved wife goodbye.

CHAPTER 2

Time to Serve

J ames was only 10 when his mom died. Now the years went by, and he is now 19, Jack 20 and Vinny 21 and they are eager to serve their country. It was April 8, 1933. Around the time Hitler became chancellor of Germany. The Depression was starting; the stock market crashed a few years earlier in 1929. The country was out of work. It was everywhere, even the Southside of Chicago. Ralph got laid off, and no money was corning in. James decided to enlist, but in which branch: Navy, Marines, Army? "What?" he said to himself. Which one? they were becoming men now they decided what branch to serve in. Jack Joined the Airborne division he went to Fort Benning, Ga. Vinny decided to Join The Tuskegee at Tuskegee Institute, Then to Moton airfield in Alabama James had to make his own decision now. No mom or dad beside him to tell him what to do. His father was homeless and living in shelters while James was on his way to enlist.

He drove his dad's truck that his father couldn't bear to sell because of his memories of his wife, Julia, and of her being beside him in that old truck. He couldn't bear to sell it, so he gave it to James. James slept in it, drove it everywhere. When he came across an airfield, he saw a pilot going into a double-wing plane, and that's when he decided on an army air corps. "I want to be a mechanic and pilot someday," he said. He enlisted, went into the academy air force base in Pensacola, Florida. He went to school to learn how to build engines, then he learned how to fly them. He was an ace, knew all the studs, barrel rolls, dive tactics; he was the best. Came out first in his class, second lieutenant. Other classmates in his school were eager to fly with him, wanted to be his wingman. He was the best.

Several years later, he went by his old neighborhood and found his dad in a homeless shelter. He brought him to Florida where he was stationed, set up a room for him in one of the officers' homes. They took good care of his dad, watched him while James was away on training. James was at his peak; he was ready to serve anywhere there was going on. So he enlisted to go fight in the South China Sea against a foe that would haunt him through the Second World War, the Japanese.

It was June 6, 1936. He was now first lieutenant and now flying with this squadron known as the Sky Hawks squadron of brave men volunteering their service, Part the flying Tigers 23rd fighter group the Japanese aggression over China. Their names were (Marine corps) Major Paul Millstone, (Marine corps) Captain Nick Washburn, (Army air corps) First Lieutenant James Stern, (Marine corps) Second Lieutenant Tony Lambert, and (Army air corps) Second Lieutenant Duane McSwaine (Navy)Lt JG George Wilton (Navy)LCDR Rick Ashford these men separate from rest of the group.

They fought endlessly against Japanese Zeros as they became good friends. All of them looked at James as a leader because Major Paul Millstone was shot down. Captain Nick Washburn got wounded Because of his aggressions, that was when they nicknamed him Sky Hawkins. After all, who was better in the sky than James Stern in the Sky Hawk Squadron.

Japanese were losing Zeros every hour thanks to Sky Hawkins, but one day, the tables turned. Sky and his crew flew into a cloud covering, ambushed zeroed in on the SkyHawks, barely did they get away, and bullets holes on the side of the P47 Thunderbolt in every SkyHawk fighter. Only three survive on the onslaught of machine-gun fire ripping the tail end of the P47. The Sky Hawks were done.

Sky and Duane barely made it back to base engines on fire, their canopy shattered as they barely landed in Singapore, which was held by the British Government. Sky, Duane and Nick caught an American freighter back to the States where they took R&R and became best friends.

Sky went back to Florida to see his dad, and Duane went back to Bristol, Connecticut, where he lived with his dad. Sky met an army nurse, took good care of his dad. Her name was Elizabeth Washburn,(Nick's sister) in the army hospital where his dad was in. Sky's father was ill, not caring about his health after Julia, the love of his life, died. He died of pneumonia in the army hospital in Pensacola, Florida, on November 17, 1938, at the age of forty.

Italy

Location: Italy is a country in southern Europe. It is a boot-shaped peninsula that extends into the Mediterranean Sea. Italy is bordered by France, Switzerland, Austria, and Slovenia.

Capital: Rome is the capital of Italy.

Size: Italy covers 116,306 square miles (301,230 sq km), including the islands of Sicily and Sardinia.

Population: The population of Italy is about 57,634,300 (as of July 2000).

Flag: Italy's flag is made of three equal-sized rectangles of red, white, and green. The green is by the flagpole.

Other countries located within Italy: San Marino is located within Italy near the eastern coast. The independent Vatican City (Holy See) is located within Rome.

Climate: Italy mostly has a mild, Mediterranean climate. The far north is cold and mountainous; the south is rugged, hot, and dry.

Major rivers: The major rivers in Italy are the following: the Po River (which flows from the Alps near the French border, through Turin, and eastward into the Adriatic Sea), the Arno River (which flows from the north-central Apennines, through Florence, and into the Tyrrhenian Sea), and the Tiber River (which flows from the north-central Apennines, south through Rome, and into the Tyrrhenian Sea).

Mountain ranges: The Alps are a mountain range located along the north of Italy. The Apennines are another mountain range that runs through the center of Italy.

Highest point: The highest point in Italy is Mont Blanc, in the Alps on the border of Italy and France. Mont Blanc (Monte Bianco) is 15,770 feet (4,807 m) tall.

Lowest point: The lowest points in Italy are at sea level (the level of the Mediterranean Sea).

Sky deeply regretted not taking care of his father more after his mother's death. It was too hard for the both of them after Julia's accident january 1928. She made a big impact on both of their lives. She was their life, so now Sky was really depressed knowing his dad passed away. He started drinking more heavily than usual. He got married to Elizabeth Washburn on February 25, 1939 in the army chapel in Pensacola, Florida, his close friends attended Nick, Duane, other officers and friends of Sky and Elizebeth it was a small ceremony at the base chapel Sky knew his drinking took a toll on their marriage. He would come in late, drunk, and argued. She wanted a divorce. They both went to Italy for the vacation, and that was where she met captain Hans Grenchmen of SS while Sky was at Naples to visit Al Pasqual.

A friend he knew in the states, Joe owner and retail in Produce with 2 other Brothers And a sister Carmella was (the accountants and secretary for their business) Sal and Al, was in shipping Produce all over Chicago when James was a teen; he got him a job in Al Produce on Manor Avenue on the Northside of Chicago. As Sky visited his old friend, Elizabeth was at Hans Grenchmen's (Mueller) estate in Milan. She was in love with the German officer's handsome blond hair and blue eyes, with that German accent. Sky stayed at a villa in Naples knowing Elizabeth did not want him to go back to the hotel. So he and Al hung out and drove around Italy while Elizabeth was sleeping with Hans.

Finally, a week went by, and Sky knew his leave was almost over, and he needed to get back to the States by Monday. It was now Saturday, and he needed to get Elizabeth and head back home. By the time he got back to the hotel, Elizabeth already checked out and moved in with Hans. Sky found the note left at the front desk. She said, *James, I had enough of you, and our marriage is no longer. The six months was the hardest, you being away and your aggressive drinking, I no longer can take it. Love, Elizabeth.*

Sky wasn't surprised by this marriage going downhill. He married her out losing his father, felt guilty, and also his mother's death that he carried in his mind and heart for a long time. So he left her in Italy and headed back to the States. When he got back to Pensacola,

Florida, he got a message stating *I'm living in Milan with German Officer I met when you were in Naples. Love, Elizabeth*. Short and sweet, Sky replied angrily, crumbled the letter, and threw it away. Their marriage only lasted six months.

Next morning, Sky got up, and a call came from General Grimwall, commander of the base, telling him, "Sky, you've been promoted to captain, and you have a new plane to be assigned, to the *Phantom*." Sky looked at this new plane, found out it was broken down and needed a lot of care, and Sky knew he was the man to do it. After all, he always loved to repair planes, so he painted the emblem of the patch he wore in South China: the hawk carrying a thunderbolt in remembrance of his falling airmen.

Meanwhile At 178 Wilson road in Bristol, Connecticut, Duane came home to see his father sitting in his chair, listening to the president's fireside chat. "Hi, Dad, how is it going?"

"Hi, son, glad to see you back, must have been tough over South China Seas," Mr. McSwaine replied.

"Yeah, Dad, we lost so many good men. Sky, Nick and I are the only ones to return from there. Dad, I'm just glad to be home with you and relax, play some golf, go to the movies, catch a Red Sox game, and just want to get some R&R," Duane replied.(July 7 1915 Duane Elton McSwaine was born in Bristol General Hospital went Lutheran St Matthews Elementary on Eastwood Avenue then went to Bristol High(home Lancers) on Kings Street loves the Red Sox ice hockey baseball pool and bowling and fishing his favorite pastime around golf any chance he can with his father and brother Kevin)

A year passed since the Indo China War, Duane's dad became ill, caught pneumonia that winter and died at the age of fifty. Mr. Jonathan William McSwaine was buried in Bristol, Connecticut, at All Saints Cemetery. Duane's family were of Scottish and Irish and German background, their faith Lutheran, his mom Margret everyone knew her as (peggy) pass away from breast cancer at age of 36 a couple years earlier(he Join up to help his dad with bills Duane too like Sky tried to support his father being out of work during the depression)everyone attended. Sky flew up from Florida and landed his Piper J-3, Cub (his company logo on the side)at

Rentschler Field in East Hartford to attend. Mr. McSwaine's funeral in Bristol with friends and family gather at his father's home that evening. that'sWhen he asked Duane "When is the right time you can come live with me in Palm Beach Florida" Duane said, "Sounds great! Thanks, Sky, for the offer." That spring, Duane sold his Dad's house and moved to Palm Beach FL where Sky lived.

CHAPTER 3

South America Bound

The date was October 9, 1938, two years after the French Indochina war!

The Aircorps pay wasn't cutting it so he decide he had borrowed money from the(Chicago mob that his friend Joe recommend when he got his produce business started on Northside of Chicago few years earlier) at the time he was desperate to buy his own business with no banks, won't lend him money because he had no collateral and now he was celebrating his twenty-fourth birthday at his private country club in Burlington, Vermont, with a few of his close friends. One of his employees, Frank Potier, was driving up from Sky's airport in Rutland. Sky became one of the largest airports in the northern parts of New England. The company was called Sky-Way Cargo. Their slogan was "Go our way, Sky Way, We Never Delay! We import and export from available portraits to rare exotic fruits and assorted nuts and pistachios, plants, birds, and animals, nothing is too large or small, that we can't handle." that's when the money started rolling in he paid the mob off with high interest rate to boot he borrow at the time 50,000 and he had pay back 150,000 to the mob a few months back.

When Frank arrived at his destination, to the Sky-Way Cargo. It had a huge large airfield and hangers. Sky had a clubhouse with a bar and rooms to sleep and a billiard room he had for his employees to relax, enjoy themself and a huge office with shutter doors in the back of the billiard room. "Why doesn't he ever invite me to any of his gatherings?" Frank asked himself.

He buzzed the intercom; a deep voice answered. "Yes, may I help you?.

"Hey, Derek, it's me, Frank! Let me in, I've got a letter here marked urgent for Sky!"

"Hang on for a minute, I'll buzz you in the front gate!"

"Okay," Frank replied as he waited patiently for the buzzer to open the gate. He put the Jeep in gear, and it stalled. "Stupid Jeep!" he said in anger. "I've got to get that carburetor fixed." He started up again and stepped on the gas, posthaste this time. And the Jeep rattled up the long, winding driveway.

Sky waited for him at the front door of his exotic club. Frank gave him the letter marked "Urgent" on it as he looked up to Frank. That's when he asked him. "Frank, what's wrong, you look frustrated!"

"Oh, it's nothing, the Jeep stalled on me again coming up here, Sky, that's all."

"Well, come on in and fix yourself a drink, follow me into the billiard room, okay." Sky smiled as they both walked into the billiard room. Sky had just finished up his game with his first-class mechanic John Bass.

He told him and his other buddies to excuse him as he was opening up the letter with his pocket knife that he reached for in his pants pocket As Sky was reading the letter, he could hardly hear himself reading, so he told his friends to leave so he could finish reading the letter in peace, and so they left, closing the door behind them. Sky sat on the pool table reading the letter, sipping his Jack Daniel's and Coke.

"Hey, Sky! This is your old-time friend Leon".

"I have a proposal for you if you are interested in going on a little trip with me to Peru in South America."

"I'm offering you a lifetime of wealth if you come with me."

"I'm after the biggest find ever! For a museum, since the discovery of King Tut's tomb! That's why I can trust only you, because I know you can keep this confidential, so please call me at this number at ten o'clock tomorrow night I'll be expecting your call! I owe you one!"

Signed, your old friend Doctor Leon LeClere, Archeologist.

Now, it's Sunday night, ten o'clock just rolling around. Sky picked up the phone and started dialing. The phone started ringing.

"Hello," the voice answered.

"Leon!" Sky replied.

"Yes," the voice answered.

"This is Sky Hawkins. You mailed me a letter stating you needed my help, referring to a golden idol in South America, I imagine."

"Yes, yes," Leon replied. "Please hurry down here, please!" he said in a nervous voice!

"Okay, okay. Where the hell are you?"

"I'm in Florida, Miami, Florida!" I'm being followed by an unmarked car with four guys in it. I'll meet you at this destination. Write it down, Sky, write it down."

"Okay, I'm writing it down. Where?"

"It's in 1867 Ocean Boulevard, in the tavern called Hanna's Sunset Grill. I'll be there in two days. I have to get my son, Johnny. I left him in the hotel not too far away from here because I'm not too sure what I am up against here, okay! Gotcha. I'm leaving now. see you tomorrow, okay! Goodbye." And they both hung up.

Sky turned to Frank and said, "We are heading south tonight to Hanna's Sunset Grill on Miami beach. So let's go, Frank." Sky told his guests, "I'm sorry, but the party's over for me. I have a job to do, and it can't wait. So please excuse me and stay here as long as you like. I'll try to be back here on Friday, so take care, guys."

"Hey, where are you going?"

"Hanna's Sunset Grill down on Miami Beach 1867 Ocean Blvd.," he said as they were heading out the door. as Dr. Leon Leclerc hang the phone up he headed out to get to get his son Johnny at the Flamingo Resort Hotel downtown, Miami as he was getting to the car to go to the Flamingo Resort Hotel in downtown, Miami As he was being followed by a black buick he notice 4 men getting out he started to run inside the Hotel and ran up 5 flights of stairs until he reach his room he bang on the door yelling out frantically, Johnny hurry we must go now!" as Johnny unlocked the door to let his father scream nervously hurry get your things son we must leave now!" as Johnny confused and panicking said what is wrong! father is wrong! as Johnny hurry grab his things ran out of the room with his father not far behind him. he told" Johnny go down fire escape and head for the nearby police station" "ok father" as he ran down the fire escape as he heard shots being fired and look up and see his dad falling off the fire escape to the streets below!Sin pointed out at the boy told his henchmen go get him they ran down after him as the boy made his way to the streets and noticed Duane coming out of the restaurant on Dolphins blvd! he ran to him crying look up at Duane and crying my father is dead Duane my father is dead! as Duane looked down at Johnny and said 'Who did this brutal crime who was that evil to do a thing like that!" Duane said angrily and then told Johnny to come with him he will be safe! Meanwhile Sin put Dr. Leclerc in the trunk of the car with Dr. Cook body that he murder few hours before as his henchmen putting the body in the trunk they noticed the boy left with Duane in his green pickup truck and reported back to Dr. Sin henchman reported back that the boy is with some man with a red baseball cap and a brown flight jacket they drove off in a green pick up truck heading north. Sin told them" let them go, we got the map now! that will lead us to the golden idol" that is when he started to laugh! "Let's head back to the keys and let Col. Wolfenstien have the map now we can proceed on our mission for the fuhrer! meanwhile Duane got home to call Sky to warn him about the plot to be unfold but it was too late Derek pick up and explain to Duane and said "Sky had left hours ago to Miami to see the good Doctor" "ok I heading to pick up your brother Dustin at fort Benning and head down to Peru" Duane replied. "ok Derek replied" and take care of yourself and tell my crazy brother to watch out stay safe hope see him soon in Atlanta thanks Duane take care bye" as both hung up so off he went to meet Major Larson he flew down in a piper plane J-3 cub Sky's other piper to Atlanta, Ga he called Dustin once he arrived told him meet him at the airport Dustin agree happy to help his good friends Duane and Sky and (Dustin agreed to meet Johnny and found out what the mission all about retrieving the golden idol for Johnny) after his two weeks training at 82th airborne Division in fort Benning. So two weeks later they went to Eglin Airfield then Duane got clearance to take a C-47 cargo plane as Major Lawson in copilot seat as push the throttle forward as the rudders pedals made the rudders moved up and down as they got go head to take off on runway 6 and off they went airborne as Duane and Dustin, Johnny headed for Peru! meanwhile back in Miami, Sky turned and told Frank to "leave the Jeep here and we'll take my car," a 1938 Silver Jaguar SS 100.

As soon as he got there, they both jumped into his twin-engine plane and flew down to Miami, and from there, they took a taxi to the hotel where Leon was going to be. The following night, they left for Hanna's Sunset Grill on 1867 on Ocean Boulevard. Sky and Frank were sitting in the bar, drinking a beer. It was about nine o'clock that evening. The bar was pretty crowded. Soon someone said, "Hanna's, serving banana daiquiri," and Dennis Westport Hanna bartender want buy around for the house because it was Hanna one year anniversary having her own business so Dennis decide buy and before they knew it, everyone was getting a second round of the house specialty "The Hanna's banana daiquiri" on the house.

In the meantime, someone was calling out his name. "Hey, Sky, Sky Hawkins," the voice yelled from a distance, but Sky did not recognize the voice.

"Yo, over here!" Sky replied as the two men shuffled their way through the crowds. Sky waved them on.

One man said as they approached Sky, "He is waiting in the car for you. He changed his mind about coming in because look how crowded it is."

The man with the dark complexion said, "Come, come with us. We will show you where he is."

Frank looked up to Sky as he was standing in front of the two men, and Sky turned around, looking down at Frank as he was about to get up from his chair. Sky looked at Frank, puzzled, like what the hell is going on here! As the two men pointed the way out the door, they started to follow Sky and Frank toward the door. As they stepped out, they noticed a black 1934 Buick. Offhand Sky couldn't think of the name of the Buick, but it had suicide doors.(1936 Buick Century) All four men got into the car and drove off. They were heading toward the Keys. Sky was getting suspicious. He kept asking the man in the backseat with him and Frank where Dr. LeClere was. He kept asking the man as he looked out the window saying, "Don't you worry, you will see him soon enough" as they drove down the old back road, bumpy as it could be.

Finally, they reached their destination. They all got out of the car. There were six men altogether, including Sky and Frank. They reached a mansion. It was white and had four pillars holding the roof up. The house was built in the early 1800s. They could hardly see the house through all that heavy fog that was rolling in. There was a full moon even though some clouds were hiding it. You could barely see it over the house. It looked kind of eerie from a distance, with a large willow tree hanging over on both sides of the house.

As they opened the door, they noticed a tall man with blonde hair and blue eyes with a monocle in one eye, smiling and saying, "Good evening, come in, come in!"

"Yeah, yeah," Sky replied, puzzled as he could be, and he said to the gentleman, "Where is Dr. LeClere, where is he? I was supposed to meet him in Miami over four hours ago. Where is he?"

"In due time, my friend, in due time!" the blonde-haired man replied with a laugh.

At that moment, another strange man came through a double sliding door. As he was shutting them behind him, he smiled and said, "Welcome, welcome."

"Yeah, yeah, we heard from your pal already. For the last time, where is Dr. LeClere?" Sky replied.

"Oh, yes, the good doctor. You'll see him soon. Step this way, gentlemen, in the study, and have a drink with me."

As all four men walked into the study, they noticed the room was gloomy, hardly any lights in it. As the man fixed the boys their drink, Sky noticed the Swastika on the man's lapel. As the man was giving them their drinks, he looked right at Sky Hawkins and said, "Is scotch and soda good enough, or would you like it with bourbon?"

Sky looked shocked, wondering how the hell he knew what he liked. "I never met this guy before!" he said to himself as he was given the drink. "Who are you and what do you want?"

As the two men started laughing again, the man with Swastika on his lapel was looking at a book and slammed it on his desk, which scared the hell out of Frank. He turned around, looking right into Sky Hawkins's face and said, "My name is Colonel Wilhelm Wolfenstien of the SS, and I am here to get the golden idol for my führer, and you and your friends are not going to stop me now. What do you think of that, my friends?"

Sky looked at him and threw his drink right into his face and pulled out his .45 and shot the other SS officer right in the head as he was reaching inside his coat pocket. He told Frank to get the hell out of there; as Frank opened the sliding door, he was sprayed by machine-gun fire. Sky dived through a stained-glass window that led him into another room, as Wilhelm, wiping his face with anger and said to his henchmen, "Kill him now!" They were shooting the hell out of the room. Sky barely got out of the way of stray bullets. He burst through another window that led him outside. He rolled around on the grass, got up with minor cuts and bruises, wiping himself off from the debris of wood and glass that was on him as he held on to one leg, making his way into the muddy swamps of the Everglades.

The Germans started toward the back of the house looking for Sky. That's when The Colonial called them back in Germans and said the alligators would get him. "Let's get to the plane and fly to South America with our good doctor."

As Sky was making his way through the swamps, he noticed his leg was bleeding. He stopped to lean against an old willow tree and ripped open his right pants leg and noticed a big gash in his right leg. He started to scream as he pulled the glass out of the gash. Blood was pouring like water as he tried to tie a piece of cloth around it, saying to himself, "Why me, Lord, why me?"

Meanwhile, the 20 Germans made their way to Key Largo, where a plane was waiting for them.(CL-215 amphibious flying boat) The pilot started the plane; she puttered around the water's edge and finally headed south toward Peru, riding rough to the open sea. The pilot lifted her up toward the sky, and off they went. Sky at that time was feeling weak, afraid that he might wind up dying out here. He started to get up, felt dizzy, and then he collapsed forward and fell unconscious.

Five minutes later help arrived. Two poachers came by and spotted Sky lying on his belly, bleeding to death.

One wanted to leave him, but the other said, "No, we can't, look at him, he's helpless. Besides, look at his leather jacket. He is an army corps pilot, like my father." The two boys picked him up and carried him to the pickup truck. The oldest boy was sixteen. He drove Sky to the nearest hospital for treatment.

A week went by, and Sky was regaining consciousness. Things were still blurry. He shut his eyes as the light was starting to bother him.

"Where the hell am I?" he asked loudly.

"Shhh," the nurse replied. "You are in a hospital."

"How did I get here?" Sky replied.

"Two boys brought you in, they said they found you lying on the side of the road."

"No, I wasn't, I was somewhere in the Everglades at the time. I remember Germans. I was fighting Germans," Sky said as fell back unconscious.

The Nurse named Sharon just gave him a sedative to help him sleep better.

When Sky Hawkins came for the second time, he called out, "Nurse, nurse!"

She came running in. "Yes, what is it! Are you alright?" she asked.

"Where am I?" he asked for the second time.

"You are here at the hospital. I told you that the last time you asked!" she replied.

"Who brought me here. Last I remember, I was in the swamps somewhere."

"Yes, I know, you told me that! I told you two boys brought you in. Don't you remember?"

"No, I don't remember anything."

"You were mumbling about some Germans and then I gave you a sedative to put you back to sleep.

"Germans? Germans, let me recall. Oh yeah. Frank! Frank is dead! The Germans killed Frank! They must have kidnapped Dr. Leon LeClere. Oh yeah, now I remember. That's right, I must get out of here right now!" Sky said.

The nurse shook her head no and said, "The doctor must check you out."

Sky Hawkins looked in dazed bewilderment as he tried to get up. Finally, he made it up and slowly made his way to the corridor.

Meanwhile, nurse Sharon was calling for a doctor to help her get Sky back to bed.

But Sky kept pushing her away as he put on his pants and shirt and socks and shoes and told nurse Sharon I am ok my leg hurts a little that all grabbed his flight Jacket and left, made it to the nearest exit. Finally, he made it outside as the nurses and doctor were calling for him to come back.

As a bus pulled up beside the hospital to let off passengers, Sky climb up small step into the bus.

Meanwhile, the bus pulled away from the hospital as the nurses and doctors stood by and watched.

Back on the bus sky put dine in the slot and hop to his seat and took a sleeping pill nurse gave him to take earlier he had in his left jacket pocket as he fell asleep to ease the extreme pain.

The bus driver looked at him wondering to himself what happened to him.

as bus stop at the bus station pick up more passenger he woke up Sky and said "where at the train station you like get off here buddy"

As he got down, off the bus he as he rubbing his right leg and felt the stitches and said to himself, "I must get them out as soon as possible.: Then he made his way to a train station and went inside to rest on a bench for a while and fell asleep to escape the pain.

An hour went by, and a policeman nudged him. "You can't sleep here, buddy, you must go now!"

Sky got up very slowly because of the extreme pain, and in a daze he made his way slowly toward the train tracks. The police officer, helping Sky off the tracks, said, "That's not the way, buddy. Out the front exit. Do you want me to call an ambulance."

"No, no!" Sky replied. "I'm fine. Thanks." And he once again found his way back to the street, wondering which way to go. He made his way to the center of town and noticed a black and yellow van, with a sign saying "Air Transport." He said to himself, "Maybe I can get a lift to the airport with this van."

Sky limped to where the van had stopped and opened the passenger door and asked the driver if he could get a lift to the nearest airport.

The man looked amazed and said, "Sure, no problem, get in. You caught me just in time. I was heading back at this time!"

"Great," Sky replied Sky and the man made small talk. Sky asked him his name, and the man replied, "Bill, Bill Jackson but my friends called me Duke' What's yours?"

Sky, with extreme pain, replied, "Sky Hawkins."

"Hey, buddy, you get that leg checked out?"

"I already did, and it's fine. My leg will heal sooner or later," Sky replied.

"Why are you going to the airport? Flying somewhere special?" Bill asked.

Why, as a matter of fact, I am. Peru, why do you ask?"

"Oh, no special reason, I was just wondering, that's all."

And suddenly, Sky fell off to sleep again.

Bill finally made it to Miami Municipal Airport. (it was being used byThe British for military training) Bill shook Sky, trying to wake him up.

"Sky, wake up," Bill said, "we're here at the airport."

Sky looked up and out the window and said, "Great, thanks. I owe you one, Bill!"

And he turned and smiled and shook his hand and, just as he tried to open the van door, Bill turned and said "glad to meet you Sky take care of yourself hope see you again bye."

"Ok, Bill, I really appreciate that, take care as he shook his hand and got out of the van!" off he went heading toward the entrance to the airport, waving back at Bill.

That's when Bill took off from the airport after taking on more passengers back to the hotel.

Meanwhile, Sky walked past the military personnel and headed toward the main gates, where he believed his twin-engine might be.

One MP stopped him and said that he couldn't go beyond the gate. "Authorized personnel only. Can't you read the sign?"

Sky shook him off and started limping toward the field. The MP yelled to other MP's, "Hey, stop that man, he's not allowed on the field."

Sky was hoping desperately, holding his right leg as he made his way to his plane with no time wasting. He started her up, and down the runway he went. He pushed the throttle forward, pulled the steering wheel back, and up he went, looking down and waving goodbye. He made a sharp right-hand turn, and off he went, heading toward South America.

Sky landed in an open field 6 hour later, His plane spun around until he came to a full stop, and he got into the back of the plane to grab his B.A.R.(Browning Assault Rifle)and some grenades and headed to the jungle. He was walking through, making a path, then he came across a hanging bridge. It swayed side by side. He had to be five hundred feet from the river below as he crossed it; he could see the other side of the mountains. He finally made it across the other side. He started to follow the path again, then finally made it to a cave inside. He could hear Germans say they had the golden idol. They put it in their pouch and headed toward the airfield where Duane and Dustin, Johnny, and were being watched from the jungle by Indians got there eight hours before Sky did track down Golden

Idol and spotted the Germans and Dr. Won Sin, and that's when all hell broke out in the airfield.

Major Larson and Lieutenant McSwaine and the Quechua Indians reached the airfield where the C-46 cargo plane was parked, just as Dr. Won Con Sin, Colonial Wolfenstein and Major Mueller, and Captain Grenchmen and 3 german Infantry men arrived in CL-215 amphibious aircraft. drop them off, spun around and headed back to Germany! Meanwhile Colonial Wolfenstien, Major Mueller, along with Captain Han van Grenchmen, were searching the C-46 plane for their Golden Idol! The rest of the Germans were searching the grounds. Suddenly one of the Germans spotted the Indians coming toward them and opened fire! All hell broke loose, with machine-gun fire!

Dustin and Duane rolled to the ground, bullets flying over them; they crawled toward the plane toward Dr. Sin and other officers! Meanwhile some of the Germans found their way back to the caves to hide by the waterfall by the hanging bridge as they tried to cross it. Indians started cutting the rope, and some Germans fell toward the river below, as others made their way into the cave! The Quechua Indians started throwing bamboo spares, and blow darts came flying at the unexpecting Germans, pinning two of them to cave wall; the others grabbed the Golden Idol and started back, yelling to the major in German, "We've got it, we've got it, the Golden Idol for our führer!" But before they could reach where the Colonial, Major and Captain and the 20 infantry were, Dustin and Duane went into action!

Dustin fired on them and killed them all. Sky grabbed Captain Hans Van Grenchmen as he reached for the Idol and stepped on his wrist, Sky pounding him, saying, "This one for Dr. LeClere and Dr. Cook, and this one just for me!" Sky keeps punching him over and over, blood splatters everywhere as he punches his skull in, and then twisting his neck until he is dead. Just as Major Mueller grabbed his rifle to shoot Sky, Duane shot him dead. He ran toward Sky, checking to see if he was all right. The Colonial and Dr. Sin ran toward the arriving of the JunkersJu-52 and was shot by Dustin in the leg as the rest of the Indians finished the rest of the Germans off that came when JunkersJu-52 landed and dropped off more Germans Infantry as the Colonial aboard the plane.

As the plane was taking off, the Colonial grabbed Dr. Sin's arm and dragged him into the plane as the plane started to take off. Meanwhile Dustin, Sky and Duane and Johnny made their way back to *Phantom*. Sky and Duane start the engines, as the Indians attack *The C-46* Cargo Plane, with the Indians starting to throw spares at C-46 trying to retrieve their idol.

As Sky and Duane started taking off on the open field soon they pushed the throttle forward and then pushed back on the steering wheel and Heading off into sunset back toward the States with the Golden Idol safe on Johnny lap, Johnny exclaimed, "Someday he will find, Dr. Sin, and I will kill him, for what he did: Murdering, My father. Someday! Someday!" as Major Larson tried to comfort him as they headed into the wild blue yonder!

CHAPTER 4

The Setup

Now it's two years later.

Camaguey, Cuba, December 10, 1940. Mrs. Elizabeth Lynn Grenchmen went looking for revenge for her husband's death. She recalled years ago the names of five Cubans who assassinated the prime minister of Spain ten years ago: Jose Vasguase, Roberto Diaz, Mondale Sanrana, Teto Frandese, and the notorious Neno Torras.

They escaped from Spain, were exiled to Brazil in 1930, and then returned to Havana under different names. Sanchez Qwim was also known to be an alias, but that never stopped him from getting ahead in organized crime and becoming the most powerful and richest man in drug trafficking in his time. He had long greasy black hair in a ponytail, with a patch on his left eye and a large scar that ran from the bottom of his left nostril to the bottom of his chin, and he smoked, of course, Cuban cigars. Elizabeth had to make contact with Senor Peraz, who ran a casino hotel in Camaguey. Peraz made the arrangements for her to meet Senor Torras at the Santa Maria Casino Hotel in room 226 at 10:00 PM. And so she did, and he was waiting there with his four other henchmen. She knocked on the door, and one of his henchmen answered, "Yes, senorita, may I help you?"

"Yes, I've been told that I could find Senor Torras here."

"Yes, may I ask who's calling?"

"Yes, Mrs. Elizabeth Grenchmen!"

"Come in, Mrs. Grenchmen, come in!"

She stared at this man who was standing in front of the window with his back toward her and said, "What can I do for you?"

She replied, frightened as she looked around, "I have been told that you can do me a great favor!"

"And what's that?" he asked.

"Assassinate a man for me. His name is Sky Hawkins, and I want him dead! He killed my husband, Hans van Grenchmen, have you ever heard of him?"

"No, Senorita, no, I haven't!" Senor Torras replied as he turned around to look at her.

"Well, with Sky, it was a compassionate marriage, and with Hans, we were planning to have kids. He was a Stormtrooper and a German captain too! Now do you know him?"

"No, Senorita, I still don't know him!" he answered. "It's going to cost you, Senorita."

"Yes, I know. How much?"

He started laughing as he was looking up and down at her, smiling, and said, "Take off your coat now!" And so she did, then he asked her to turn around, and she did. "Very nice figure, I want you to be my call girl. You will be working for me!" And he started to laugh out loud.

Her face turned pale, and she did not know what to say. Neno Torras walked up to her and ran his fingers through her hair and said, "Yes, you'll do just fine."

His henchmen started to laugh; she was so scared, and she knew she was in a jam. If she tried to escape, she knew they would kill her for sure. He said, "Is it a deal, Senorita, or what?"

With tears in her eyes she nodded her head yes.

And he said, "Good, you never will regret it." And he started to laugh once again. Then he spoke to his henchmen in Spanish, telling them to make the arrangements to fly to...

"Where?" he asked.

Elizabeth answered, "Palm Beach, FL. and the address is 1818 Seaville Boulevard. He owns a white duplex house with dark brown shutters, and it has a gravel driveway with a built-in pool in the back, and he has a 1939 Silver Jaguar SS 100 and 1937 Green Mercedes Benz Roadster, those cars he keeps ethier in Florida or Vermont. And his friend who lives there with Sky in Palm beach, FL his name is Duane McSwaine, he has a green 1939 Plymouth Model PT ½ ton pick up!"

"What does Senor Hawkins look like?"

"He has salt-and-pepper hair with a mustache and a dark complexion, weighs about 225 pounds, built very strong, and knows martial arts. He is a pilot in the army air corps, a captain. His friend, Duane, has dirty-blonde hair, weighs about 185 pounds, and he was a sharpshooter, and knows a little bit of martial arts. They both wear their army air corps jackets, most of the time and also have a home in Burlington, Vermont. They might be there now because it's hunting season, and they love to go deer hunting this time of the year!" Elizabeth replied.

Then he asked, "Who is he to you?"

"My ex-husband! I want him dead for what he did to me!"

Then Neno said, "No problem, no problem, don't worry, we'll get him, we'll get him!" Then he turned and told his henchmen, "Now make the necessary arrangements to go to Florida."

In the meantime, back in the States, The McSwain's was playing eighteen holes of golf at his West Palm Beach golf course with his Nephew Matthew and Duane older brother Kevin' Matthew got him by a stroke in the eighteenth hole with a hole-in-one. was an impressive way Matthew played the game Kevin and Duane taught him well! It was a two-hundred-yard stroke. It was his best drive yet. "Yes!" Matthew said, holding up his nine iron up in the air. "Now I've got you Uncle Duane!"

Duane didn't know what to say except "Good shot, Matthew, good shot!" as Kevin looked on and patted his son on the back as proud as he could be!

In the meanwhile In Burlington, Sky was having a field day of his own, clipping one moose and four white-tail deer. His hunting friends, Cliff, Eric, Derek, David, and Mario were getting hungry.

"It's getting late, come on, Sky, we've got enough, let's go!" Mario said.

"Wait one minute, I want to get one more for the record!"

"Okay, then can we go, it's nearly sunset! And we've been here since 4:00 AM!" David replied.

"Okay, okay, I'll meet you guys at the truck!" he said. Just as he finished speaking, a huge eight-point buck came out of the woods and into a patch of open fields. "Holy cow!" Sky said, "Look at that buck." He pulled back the chamber and loaded a clip. Just then, a huge grizzly charged at him.

"Look out, Sky! Lookout!" Derek yelled.

Sky turned to his right and started shooting at the huge grizzly; it did not stop him. The others fired at the bear, and finally, it fell down at Sky's feet. Sky's heart raced and he said, "Thanks, guys, I owe you one."

And they all smiled as they dragged the bear back to the truck.

As Sky and his buddies made their way back to Sky's house, they arrived about ten that evening.

The boys were pretty proud of themselves for killing that bear. That was all they talked about that evening. They ate veinason and drank beer and played a little poker. Sky and Mario just finished playing a game of pool. It was 4:00 AM, and they decided to hit the sack in Sky's guest rooms. They woke up around three Monday afternoon. Sky told them he was leaving but told them they were welcome to stay as long as they wanted, as long as they cleaned up the mess and didn't leave any ladies behind. They started laughing and said, "No problem, Sky, no problem.

When He left for Miami Municipal Airport in his Piper J-3 cub. He was thinking that his friend Duane should be waiting, since he tried to call him earlier, and he did not answer. Sky arrived at Miami around nine that evening. When he got out of the plane, he said to himself, "Boy, run, never get used to this coming from extreme cold weather up north to the hot muggy weather down here! If I keep this up, I'm going to get sick!" He took his flight jacket off and wiped the sweat off his brow. "Now where the heck is, Duane? He should have been here by now! He's never stood me up before! Where the heck is he?"

As Sky was making his way to the main gate, he ran into his friend, Dean Stone. He was on leave. He was a lieutenant commander of the *Battleship New Jersey*, waiting for his sister Elaine Stone.

"What are you doing here?" Sky asked.

"Waiting to pick up my sister coming in on a C-46 transport from the Philippines. She is a nurse, you know," replied Dean as he was laughing.

"Hey, that's great. Oh, by the way, can you do me a favor, Dean?"

"Sure, you know I owe you a few! What is it that I can do for you, Sky?"

"I need a lift home. I don't know where Duane is!"

"Okay, no problem, I hope he's alright. That doesn't sound like him to stand you up."

"I know, I know!" Sky wondered to himself what might have happened to him.

"Oh, here she comes now! Elaine, meet my neighbor, Sky Hawkins!"

"Pleased to meet you!" Sky said, smiling and shaking her hand. He noticed no ring on the ring finger of her left hand.

"Oh, it's my pleasure meeting a war hero like yourself!"

Sky smiled as his face turned red (he was blushing), and he looked down saying thanks while kicking the floor with his foot.

"I guess we should be heading home now, you guys!" said Dean Meanwhile Duane came back from playing golf with his brother and nephew" Elizabeth showed up with Toto and 5 of his henchmen Elizabeth asked Duane "where is he?" Duane "replied who are you referring to? her answer "Sky! that bastard killed my Husband!" Torras told him to 'get in the house and will wait for him!' back at the airport Sky helping Elaine Stone with her duffle bag "let me get my duffel bag and help your sister with her duffle bag."

And off they went to Palm Beach, FL making small talk.

She wanted Sky to ask her out on a date, and so he did. They made a date for Friday night at eight o'clock.

As they arrived at Sky's home, he noticed that the gate to his long driveway was open. "That's odd," he said to himself. "Duane and I always close the gate before we leave the house."

"Hey, Dean, drive by my house and pull up around the corner!"

"Sure why is there anything wrong?"

"I don't know yet, but something doesn't seem right here!"

"Okay, anything you say, Sky!" And so he pulled around the next corner and stopped.

"Dean, open up the trunk so I can get my .45 out of my duffel bag, okay!"

As Dean opened the trunk, Elaine asked, "Is there anything I can do?"

"No!" Sky replied. "Just stay in the car and keep low! Dean, drive to your house and call the police for me! Explain to them that there might be trouble at my house!"

"Okay! Sky, I'll do that! Take care and be careful, you're the only friend I have in this neighborhood! You and Duane."

Sky smiled. "Yeah, okay, just do what I ask!"

Dean took off in the car as Elaine looked toward the back window, waving goodbye with a puzzled look on her face. Sky slipped a full clip and pulled the chamber. "No one screws around with me and gets away with it!"

Sky made his way through his neighbor's yard, and then across his own yard, then he jumped the fence near the pool. He noticed three men in the kitchen with Duane. Right there he knew that spelled trouble. Duane would never have guys like them in our house. They were too greasy looking.

Sky crawled up to the side of the house, then stood up, kicked the door in, and shot the three men dead. Then he came across Duane. "What the heck is going on around here?"

And Duane explained, "That no-good low-down Elizabeth, I should have known she would be behind all of this."

"Where is she now, Duane. Where is she?"

"I overheard that greaseball Senor Torras talking to the rest of his cutthroat friends about going to Little Havana! For what, I don't know, I can't understand Spanish when they talk fast, but I'm sure they are not going down there for sightseeing!" Duane explained.

"No, I don't think so either, but I'm glad you're alright! I'm also glad you left the front gate open, or else we both will be dead right now!"

"But, Sky, I didn't leave the gate open, they must have when they left about a half hour ago. Those stupid fools!"

"Well, it worked out for the best! Let's get these scums out of our kitchen, and then we'll make a little surprise of our own when they get back!"

Suddenly the police arrived, and Duane and Sky explained the whole thing to them. They asked them not to get involved just yet because they had a score to settle. The police agreed because it would save them a lot of paperwork, and they left. Sky decided to put the corpses on the couch and a chair and told Duane to sit between them so they would look alive.

"Meanwhile I'll be behind the chair by the front door," he said. "As they come in, that's when the fireworks will begin!"

It was midnight when they heard a car coming up the driveway, and they waited.

Sky peered from the window and saw Senor Torras and Elizabeth in the car while a greaseball tried to rip open her blouse, feeling her up as they blathered. Senor Torras started grabbing Elizabeth's hair and kissing her all over while laughing. He was drunk on a quart of 151Rum!.

Elizabeth said, "Stop, you're hurting me, stop it!" As she pushed him away and started running toward the house with tears in her eyes. Torras ordered the driver to bring her back, and so the driver ran after her, and as he did, Elizabeth scratched and kicked him in the groin. That was when Sky kicked open the door. Sky started a rain of bullets and killed him instantly. Elizabeth ran back to the car, and that's when she did not realize Senor Toras was waiting for her there.

As Senor Torras started grabbing Elizabeth again, touching her hair and kissing her all over again while laughing, Elizabeth said, "Stop it, you're hurting me, stop it." She pounded on Toras chest, screaming and yelling, "Let me go, let me go!"

Sky stepped out into the front lawn and yelled at Senor Torras, "Let her go, let her go, now!"

Senor Toro grabbed Elizabeth by her hair and stuck a gun to her head (the one he had underneath his coat) and said, "I'll kill her if you try to take me, kill her, I swear!"

That's when Sky went back into the house and watched him through his picture window and then told Duane, "Keep him busy thinking that I'm here with you, while I sneak in from his blind side and pop him with this thirty aught six, from a palm tree on the side of the house."

Duane kept Torras busy, saying, "Let Elizabeth go" while Sky sneaked out and quietly stood on the side of the palm tree.

He yelled out, "Hey, monkey breath! Here I am!" As Toras turned to look, Sky shot him right between the eyes. Elizabeth started to scream, and Sky told her to shut up. That's when the police came back and arrested her for being an accomplice.

As they drove away, Sky thought it would be the last time he ever would see her again.

Sky said to Duane as they walked back into the house, "Now that's the shot that should have been heard around the world!"

They both started laughing as they made their way into the house.

"Now that's a setup, Sky Hawkins style," Duane replied.

And Sky said, "Another job well done!" And then they gave each other a high-five as they got into the living room. That's when Sky bragged about the grizzly bear he shot all by himself.

Duane said, "Yeah right, sure you did," as he shut the front door, laughing and shaking his head saying, "I can't believe I'm listening to this, you are unbelievable."

"What! What it's true, I did, ask anyone who was up there. It was at close range too!"

"Oh, please, stop it, you are making me laugh too hard, stop it! Please!"

"But it's true. Ask Dave, Cliff, Mario, Eric or Derek. They were there."

Duane was laughing hysterically as he was closing the door shut.

CHAPTER 5

A Call from Washington

I t's Sunday Morning February 16, 1941 Sky and Duane decided
to stop by Dan and Abbey Rhones Bar and Grill for a bite to
eat. At breakfast, they talk about going to the Old Town Trolley
museum in Washington D.C. they looked at the menu and decide
what they wanted for Breakfast and told(Lovely Rita) their waitress
the name Sky's calls her, her name is Rita Rhodes Dan and Abby
Rhodes daughter trying made money to pay some of the tuition
and pay for some of her books for college as they order Ham and
eggs over easy with home fries and coffee, Duane order flapjacks and
bacon orange juice and coffee then left her 20 dollar tip to help her
way through school as smiled and said WOW! thank you as she took
the bill back to the cashier.

A Month went by after the incident with Elizabeth! They took
little R & R. A week before the call from Washington, they went
deep-sea fishing and played a game of golf at Duane's West Palm
Beach golf course when they arrived home. One afternoon, the
phone rang! Sky answered, and it was a call from the White House.

"Is this Sky Hawkins?" the caller asked.

"Yes, it is," Sky replied, puzzled. "What can I do for you?"

"This is Major Walberg, you need to be in Washington, urgent
request from the president. You and Duane must be here as soon as
possible to go on a secret mission. Chief of staff will be waiting, see
you, guys. When can we expect your arrival here in Washington?"

Sky replied, "Friday at 8:00 AM, would that be fine, sir?"

"Yes, that would be fine, Captain, I'll let the chief of staff know, thank you, and good luck to both of you." Then Sky hung up and told Duane the news.

Duane was eager to serve his country; as for Sky, he was puzzled, not knowing the mission, but he said to Duane, "That is why we signed up for, let's start packing and get ready to go to DC." Sky said, shaking his head and smiling, "We are finally meeting the president."

Sky was laughing as Duane patted him on his back and said, "Let's go get ready for Washington, Sky!"

It was now Thursday Morning, and at 6:00 AM, Sky and Duane headed out in Duane's truck. They Drove to the Army Air Corp Base in Eglin, Florida, where they got onboard and flew to Langley Army Air Corps in Hampton, Virginia; They arrived at 11:00 am Thursday, got the Jeep, and headed for Washington. They got there a day earlier than expected, which was Friday at 8:00 AM, so Sky and Duane stayed at the Grandview Hotel in Washington, went sightseeing, and enjoyed the day in DC. Rocco The taxi Driver drove them anywhere they wanted to go! they went to the Old Town Trolley museum and then Lincoln Memorial then Civil war in battlefields in Fredericksburg V.A. Appomattox Court House where Lee surrendered to Grant they just enjoyed sightseeing thanks to Rocco the man knew where to go.

That night, they went to a bar, played some pool, called some fellow officers they knew, played some poker, that night at the hotel till midnight. They hit the sack and woke up at 5:00 AM Friday, ate breakfast, and then headed out to 1600 Pennsylvania Avenue NW, where the chief of staff was waiting in the Oval Office.

Sky and Duane arrived and felt proud and honored to be called to see the president! As they got into Oval Office, they both saluted the commander and chief of our great nation, President Roosevelt, who was sitting at his desk in his wheelchair and rolled up to Sky and Duane and said, "Gentlemen, I heard a great deal about your accomplishment in South China Sea, fighting those Japs. I'm proud to know you guys, and now you are up for a promotion from captain to Lieutenant Colonel Hawkins, and Duane from Second Lieutenant to Major McSwaine." Then he shook their hands on their promotion! "That's one reason why you are here, another is I have another dangerous mission for you two. You must find General O'Hara somewhere captured in the South Pacific. He knows lots of top-secrets Japs would love to get their hands on. Try to bring back to the States alive as soon as possible. That is all, thank you, gentlemen."

And both saluted the president, and they both answered, "Yes, sir," And they left the Oval Office. Down the hall as they were leaving, Sky got a bad feeling about this mission and told Duane he didn't trust O' Hara something about him! Sky didn't like and they also needed to make one stop in Africa to drop the supply off. He promised to Joe, Al and Sal Pasqual, His old friends in Chicago! So off they went heading for Cape of Good Hope to drop off supply. "Sal expected to be there; he'll be waiting for us there," Sky replied before rescuing the general. When Sky and Duane were at the Oval Office, two mean MP's did as a joke! and they tranquilize the wolf they got from a friend who was a Zookeeper from a nearby Zoo and put the wof in the back of the cargo plane without being seen by the other MP's who were patrolling the airfield when Sky and Duane climbed. Onboard, while the wolf was asleep behind the crates; they never noticed the animal. The two MP's were thinking the wolf would rip Sky and Duane apart when it woke up.

CHAPTER 6

A Date with an Angel

Five hours passed since they left Washington, DC, heading toward South Africa. It started to rain very hard, with strong thunder and lighting. The C-46 cargo plane bounced up and down, swaying from left to right. Gale-force winds blew as Sky watched the Instruments going berserk, the needle on gages bouncing back and forth. Sky tapping it The storm was picking up intensity. Sky called to Duane, "We're headed into a hurricane! Check and make sure everything in the rear of the plane is secure!"

"Okay, Sky," Duane said as he moved to the rear. He noticed a growling noise and yelled, "Sky! Sky! There's…there's a…"

"What is it, Duane! Duane! Can you hear me!" Sky called.

"There's a wolf back here!"

"What, are you nuts?" Sky replied. "What the heck would a quadruped be doing back there?"

"How the heck do I know, but he's back here!"

Sky told Duane to slowly walk back to the cockpit. "Whatever you do, Duane, don't startle it!"

"No problem," Duane replied. Shaking like a leaf, he started walking to the front of the plane backward, his eyes looking straight into those of the wolf's. Putting his right hand on the interior wall of the plane, he watched the wolf as he felt his way back to his seat. As soon as he got back, he felt nauseous.

With fear in his eyes, he asked Sky, "What the heck are we going to do, we're between the eye of a hurricane and a wild animal?"

"I'll think of something, I'll think of something," Sky repeated over and over. Then he asked Duane, "Are you all right now?"

"Yeah, I think so," Duane replied. Duane asked Sky, "Why is it that every time I do anything with you, my life is always in danger? Can you answer that, Sky?" He said that with a smart smirk on his face.

"That's easy to answer, when I got my divorce about a few years ago, my ex-wife said, 'If you want the car or house, your life will be miserable as long as you live!' Who owns the car and the house?"

"You do?" Duane asked.

"Of course, does that answer your question, Duane?"

"Yeah."

And they both started to laugh.

Suddenly the wolf crawled right up between them and scared the hell out of Duane. Sky was laughing even harder now, with tears in his eyes as he flew into the storm. Sky bent his arm down and started petting the wolf.

"Good boy, good boy." Duane kept starting to call him "Lobo, Lobo." (Duane knew a little Spanish from his days in Mexico where he use to visits his Nephew Matthew at the time when he went to school in El paso)

Sky said, "That's it! We'll name him Lobo, Spanish for wolf."

"Hey, look, Sky, it's starting to clear, and the Instruments is working again!"

"That makes my day!" Sky replied with a grin on his face. "You know what that means, it's scotch time!"

Duane headed to the rear of the plane to grab a bottle from the cargo. Just after they finished their drink, Duane happened to look to the right out the cockpit window and noticed and pointed to the window and said. "Bogeys at 4 o'clock."

"are you sure?, "yes!" Duane replied, I'm not going to take any chances. I'm going into cloud cover until they pass!" Sky looked at Duane and started dropping his speed as he dove into the clouds. The German bogeys(it was 6 focke wulf fw-190)flew right over them, and Sky headed the plane east by southeast as Duane read the coordinates from the map to Sky.

"I believe we'll be there in forty-five minutes," Sky explained.

Cape of Good Hope was where they would land the plane in the nearest field in township S.A.and make repairs. Here they would change cargo from whiskey to Koodoo, Kola, and Koroseal. Sky figured it would take about a week.

"Hey! Sky," Duane asked, "want to go to some caves and see some stalactites and stalagmites in the Congo? Watch out for the Bago Bays up there. They are a very dangerous Pygmy tribe."

Sky asked Sal Pasqual to watch the wolf for them as Sal unloaded the cargo from the plane into Joe's warehouse.

Sal said, "Okay." He knew Sky and Duane from many years of doing business with them.

They went into the thick, dark jungle. Sky and Duane cut their way through the jungle with their machete.

"Hey, Sky, does this remind you of any place?"

"Yeah, Peru, 1938" Sky replied. "Duane! Stop for a minute and listen. Do you hear it?"

"No, hear what?"

"Gunshots! Listen very carefully, you can hear it in the distance."

"Oh yeah, where is it coming from?" Duane asked.

"I don't know, but it's getting louder. Look!" Sky looked down the path.

"It's a woman, Sky, a beautiful woman!"

Sky couldn't believe his eyes as she came up the trail. "Wow, she even knows how to handle a high-power rifle, I've got to meet her!"

Sky and Duane ran down the trail to meet her.

"Hello, my name is James Micheal Stern but everyone knows me as Sky Hawkins and this is my friend Duane Elton McSwaine. What is your name, Angel Face?" Sky said eagerly.

"Helen Joyce Seaman," she responded.

"Hello there, Helen, what a pretty name and how quaint-looking you are."

"I'll bet you say that to all the girls you meet," she said.

Duane started laughing. Then Sky said, "I think you have a great sense of humor. Where are you from?" he asked, flirting with her.

Sky Hawkins Flight Manifest (Flight Charts)

Maps of Distant Maps
This is the inventory to his manifest

Quantity	Item	Price/Value
20	Kakemono—Japanese wall picture painted on silk	$300.00
15	Kestrel—a small fakon of reddish color common in Europe and some parts of Asia and Africa (A bird)	$100.00
5	bundle Karakid—skins from Chinese goat	$50.00
3	KaraKul—sheep skins from Asia The curly black coat of new lamb	$75.00
100	bushel Kava—a variety of pepper plant native to South Pacific Island an intoxicating drink made from the macerated roots of this plant	$22.00 per bushel
25	Kaka—a parrot of New Zealand, olive brown with crimson	$5.00 a bird
5	Kakapo—a large flightless parrot of New Zealand	$750 a bird
6	plants Valerian—any herb of genus Valeriana, or the sedative drug derived there From	$100.00 a plant
100	boxes or 10 crates Vair—a fur obtained from a variety of squirrel with gray back and white belly, formerly in great demand for expensive apparel	$200.00 a crate
1	priceless vial—it's like a vessel or glass bottle (no price tag) from Indonesia	5 boxes

2	Ewer—it's like picture or a jug, it's also priceless (no price tag) from Ping dynasty	
1	Indra—a great God in Vedic mythology (priceless, no price tag) from India	
50	boxes/3 crates Pina cloth—a textile woven with fibers of the pineapple plant	$75.00 a box
1	crate decanter—a vessel used to hold decanted liquors	$25.00 a bottle

She said with a huge smile on his face, "I'm from Union City, New Jersey."

"Oh, yeah!" Duane replied. "What a small world this is!"

"What about you, Romeo, where are you from?" she asked as they walked up the trail. She had her rifle strapped to her shoulder. It was turning dusk, and she was in a hurry to get back to the hotel.

She was hot, tired, and hungry. She had been hunting all day. Sky asked Duane to leave them alone so he could get to know her a little better. Duane excused himself, saying he had to check the cargo from the plane and left them alone.

Sky said, "Now, what did you ask me? Oh yeah! Where do I live? Well, I live in Florida, Palm Beach." He said, "I also have a summer home in Vermont and a 1938 Silver Jaguar SS 100." He said, trying to impress her, "In Burlington, Vermont on Lake Champlain we can water ski and fish. I have a 25 in long shaft outboard motor boat sweetheart!

"Do you enjoy hunting?" Sky asked.

"Yes, I do very much," Helen replied. "I love going on safari for big games, I also have a boat called the Rosewood, its chris craft! In Wildwood.

"Wow," Sky said. "So what else do you like to do?"

"Scuba diving," she said.

"Oh, you're a frog lady?"

"Yeah, something like that!"

"Boy, you're not only quaint, but you're adventurous too! I like that in a woman! Are you single?"

"Maybe," she replied.

"Well, are you?" Sky asked.

"Why are you asking me all these questions!' asked Helen.

"I'd like to see much more of you, angel face! Where are you staying?" asked Sky.

"Please stop asking me so many questions! I have to go now!"

"Wait!" he yelled. "I want to get to know you even better, how about a date?"

"I'll be at the Cabana, a restaurant and casino, around eight tonight!"

"Can I make reservations for two?"

She turned and smiled, waved, and nodded her hand. "We'll see!" And walked away.

Sky was smiling and watched as she got into her Jeep and drove away. He asked Duane to make other plans because he had a date with an angel.

At eight that evening, Sky dressed in a white dinner jacket, silk black trousers, and white shirt with red bow tie. He was at the restaurant bar, sipping a scotch. He looked in the full-length mirror and saw her standing there in the archway. "Wow, how beautiful she looks!"

She wore a long black silk dress, the string of which tied at the back of her neck, a strand of pearls bedecked her smooth tan skin, and a red bow added color to her hair. And a short mink jacket hung from her arm. It was a Kolinsky. She wore French perfume that would linger in Sky's mind forever.

Sky put down his scotch, walked over to her, and asked, "Would you like to have a cocktail first?" He wondered to himself if she drank.

She said, "No, thank you, I don't drink!"

They sat down at the table by an open window and gazed upon Africa in the moonlight.

Sky told her she looked as beautiful as the evening. He gave her a rose. She smiled and thanked him. After dinner, they danced for a while, and Sky didn't want the evening to end. They talked till midnight, and she told Sky that she was a hairstylist who owned her own business in New Jersey and that this was her summer vacation.

He spoke of the fact that he was a lieutenant colonel in the army air corps and on a mission from the president.

"Wow! That sounds exciting!" she said.

It was time to leave, and Sky walked her back to her car and kissed her goodnight Then he asked, "When am I going to see you again?"

"I don't think it will be very soon, because I must go back to the States the day after tomorrow," she said.

Sky asked for her address so he could write her as much as possible. She gave the address to him, and they hugged and kissed again and spoke their goodbyes. Sky handed her a gold cross that was around his neck, in remembrance of the night. She gave him a locket with her picture of her inside. He smiled and thanked her for a wonderful evening. Helen started to walk back, as Sky waved goodbye.

Sky said to himself as he started the Jeep, "I love her." He wondered if she felt the same, as he looked at her picture inside the locket. He returned to the cargo plane with a feeling of love in his heart. This was the first time in quite some time he had felt this way.

Months went by, and the last time they were together was in Africa. Sky was preoccupied with his job running Sky Air Cargo business that he forgot to call her, then an air raid started again. German bomber hitting England for the third time, devastation all over England. Sky was in a bomb shelter as bombs dropped all over England. As planes flew over, Sky said to himself, "Thank God Helen isn't here, I must write to her soon and tell her I love her and want to see her soon.

CHAPTER 7

The Phantom Code Red

It's now March 21, 1942 11 months has passed since leaving Washington, Sky was making his way back to *Phantom* when he heard explosions coming from the dock area. "What the hell is going on!" As he reached the field, he looked for Duane and Sal Pasqual. The area was a fiery inferno Sky headed straight for his plane. Sky noticed the plane was running and ready to leave.

As he ran toward the plane, Sal yelled, "Hurry up! The Germans are coming!"

As Sky boarded, he noticed his Jeep blow up and went up in flames. He said, "Why, those no-good Krauts!" Sky made his way to the cockpit as a Kriegsmirne the F-class destroyer escorted (flottenbeglieter) zoom in on them. The explosions of the storage tanks exploding onshore could be heard behind them. Bombs fell, just missing them as they leaving the airfield made their way off the Cape of Good Hope with the destroyer in hot pursuit. firing at them they had 4.7 inch (120 mm)Mark LX guns in single mounts designated front to rear Sky and crew finally made it into the wild blue yonder once again. Sky said, "That was too close for comfort!" I want a raise after that incident!"

They flew toward French Indochina to save the general at the president's request As Sal made his way to the cockpit, Sky noticed a bird on Sal's shoulder. "What's that?" Sky asked Sal and replied, "That's my uccello!, he is falco!"

"falco!" Sky said. "nice" Sky and Duane started to look at the flight chart. Sal climb in with his falcon as the wolf snuff the bird Sal trying keep the bird calm as they took of to there next destination as Duane tell Sky the accordance to where they expect the general might be as they made their airborne again head south to southeast at 500 knot per hr wind factor 5 mile per hour clear as the can see no storms ahead 'we should get there in few hour' Sky replied to Duane "sounds right" Duane replied.

The rest of the trip was spent in silence, as Sky thought of Helen and wondered if she was safe from the Germans.

As they flew out of South Africa, away from the German F—class destroyer escort, one the cargo planes' engines started to leak oil in the left wing propeller From left to right, they started to sway. "We must have taken some flak!" said Duane.

"Yes, I can see that!" replied Sky, as the plane slowly went down.

"What's going on! What's going on!" said Sal eagerly.

"The plane got hit by flak also in the fuselage, and we're trying to land it in a safe spot," replied Duane, as he searched the map trying to find a safe place to put her down.

Sky picked up the radio and started to broadcast, "MAYDAY, MAYDAY, CODE RED." Then he turned and said, "Put on your life jackets, we're going down!" The bottom of the land gear just missed the water. They landed safely near the reef island named shoals in the South China Sea. Sky told Duane in a little while to start exploring the island.

"Hey, Sky, do you think there are any Japs on the island?" Duane asked.

"Oh, God! I hope not!"

When they got to a clear field, Sky started the repairs on the engine. "Thank God I stole some parts from the army and navy mechanics. Hey! Sal, go get my toolbox in the back of the plane. Help me take the propeller off, and hand me the gas line and that oil line."

Sal told Sky he would check the perimeter out with Duane.

Sky said, "You guys be very careful, don't run into any Japs, please! I want to get out of here within an hour."

Off Duane Sal went into the jungle with a compass, first-aid kit, and a walkie-talkie. When they reached the far side of the island, they looked around.

"Nothing," he said to himself.

Meanwhile, Sky finished installing the propeller on the cargo plane as Duane and Sal returned from the far side of the island. Sky asked Duane if he had seen any Japs.

"No," Duane replied.

"Good, let's get the hell out of here," said Sky, starting the engines of the plane, and patch up the fuselage they were ready to go, carefully checking the gauges as they left little airfield about 100 ft long the Japs must of start construction here but never finish it Sky thought to himself as they became airborne once again.

"Fuel gauges are perfect!" Duane said.

Sky told Duane "Next stop, French Indo-China! then Port Moresby then Midway Pearl Harbor then inland back to the States!". Duane marked their route on the flight chart and told Sky "got it skipper!"

March14, 1942 twenty-two hundred hours' arrival in French Indo-China airspace. "Let's circle it one time, Duane!"

"Okay, Sky!"

As they made their way, they noticed a Japanese airstrip. Not wanting to get too close for fear of being spotted.

"Hey, Sky, good thinking, we are about a month ahead of schedule now."

"Sky, can you come up with a scheme to get that general out? Without getting captured, or better yet, killed! Uh!"

"I don't know about getting killed, but I sure as hell wouldn't get captured!"

Duane engaged the hydraulics and lowered the landing gear, as they saw a field nearby where they could land.

"Hopefully no Japs will be around."

"You got it, buddy!"

Landing safely, they started to leave from the plane. Sky told Sal to stand guard, and Sal gave him some flares just in case there was any trouble, also a rifle and some grenades. Also Sal took some for himself.

Sky told Duane, "Now here's the plan, I will make a diversion at the Japanese airstrip while you get the general out at whatever cost, but be careful, you're the only true friend that I've got, and I'll never forgive myself if anything should happen to you. Got it?"

"Stop being so sentimental, Sky, it's not becoming of you, and besides, you're not with me, so I've got a better chance of survival!"

And then they both started laughing and shook each other's hand. Sky grabbed Duane, hugged him, wished him luck, and they went their separate ways.

Duane ran down the trail. He believed it would take him to where the general was. It started to get dark, so he went through it very carefully. Meanwhile, Sky was setting traps for the Japanese; he set up plastic explosives in a radar hut and on the wings of a fighter. He made sure that they were timed about five minutes apart. He was about to leave when two Japanese soldiers spotted him and tried to grab Sky. But Sky started using his martial arts. They were fighting a long time when he thought to himself, *The Germans didn't give me that much of a hard time!*

A few minutes later, the Japanese airfield exploded. Duane heard it, and said to himself, "That's my buddy Sky!" Duane finally found where he was and located the Japanese prison camp. All the Japanese were on alert after the explosion. Duane threw a grenade at a bunch of soldiers, killing most of them. He started shooting endless rounds of bullets, picking off soldiers like files. Then he got the general and about twenty other prisoners and headed back to the plane. As soon as Sky, Duane, the general and the rest of the prisoners got back, they saw a group of Japs on the plane.

"Duane, stop!" Sky called, but Duane didn't listen and crawled to the back of the plane, where he started to shoot. Sky and the rest of the prisoners were attacked. Some were killed or wounded. Duane got the plane started, and off they went. As soon as they were airborne, Sky noticed there were two more Japs aboard and started fighting again. He threw them both out as they were in the air. They must have been at 1,500 feet. Sky noticed his friend Sal Pasqual was dead, and so was his favorite wolf. He is sad for the loss of his two friends.

WWII Japanese fighter plane was called ...
shellwings.wordpress.com

Wildcat vs. Zero: How Amer...
nationalinterest.org

Myth of the Zero
historynet.com

50 Top Mitsubishi A6m Zero Pi...
gettyimages.com

A6M Zero images in 2019 | Fighter...
pinterest.com

Mitsubishi A6M Zero · Wikipedia
en.wikipedia.org

Zero fighter found in Papua New Guine...
ww2live.com

A6-M5 Zero by Mitsubishi - Japan...
aviation-central.com

Hunting Zeros | History | Air & Space ...
airspacemag.com

A6M Zero – The Deadliest ...
worldofwarplanes.eu

As they made their way to Darwin, Australia, five Japanese Zeros dove in on them. Duane noticed them first.

"Sky, look! Two o'clock bogeys!" (it was 5 Kawasaki Ki-100)

Sky tried desperately to get under the cloud cover. As the Zeros moved in, they started shooting at the C-46, putting holes in her back side.

Sky replied, "We've been hit. We're losing altitude!"

The dials on the control panel were counting down as fast as Duane could read them.

"2,000 feet, 1,500 feet, 1,100 feet," and so on.

The cargo plane was jumping up and down and making so much noise that they couldn't hear themselves speak. She was hit in the backside and pouring out one big line of smoke.

"It's hard to keep her level."

"I know that, I know! But we must try or else we're going to crash into the open sea! And I hate to be eaten by sharks."

Mitsubishi A6M Zero - Wikipedia
en.wikipedia.org

Japanese Zero Fighter Plane Flies High ...
youtube.com

World War II Zero fighter flies ov...
militarytimes.com

Mitsubishi A6M Zero WWII Japanese ...
youtube.com

Zero fighter plane being prepped...

WWII Japanese Zero A6M Zero Fig...

Zero fighter plane returns to Japa...
cnn.com

World's Only Flying A6M Zero Do...
worldwarwings.com

Zero fighter plane returns to Japan's ...
cnn.com

Mitsubishi A6M Zero ...
visitpearlharbor.org

Zero | Japanese aircraft | Britannica.com
britannica.com

CHAPTER 8

Escape to Darwin

Now it's May 18, 1942 a month after Doolittle Raid, As they just cleared the water landing in Darwin, they skidded to a stop. Both looked at each other, amazed to be alive, with only minor cuts and bruises. They got out of the *C-46* as fire engines started putting out fire to the *C-46* engines. As they made their way out of the plane, Sky and Duane shook hands as they walked away.

"Wow! That was a close one, huh, Duane!"

Sky was relieved as they walked away from death again! As both men made their way into the airport, Sky asked Duane, "Do you need to be checked out!"

Duane replied, "No! I'm okay, how about you!" As Duane looked at Sky in amazement as they were walking out of the airport and out into the streets, where they walked a bit, asking people where they could eat!

One man said, "Go to Wally's Place, great food and drinks." They shook the man's hands, and off they went. A few blocks on the left, the man pointed out and told them! "On Queen Street," he replied, "not far!" Sky and Duane said thanks and off they went. They got to Wally's, and when they got there, they relaxed and ordered their dinner.

"That was an unbelievable landing, Sky!" said Duane as he was sipping his beer and waiting to eat.

"Hey, Duane, I need to check on O'Hara and the rest of the POW, meet you at the motel around 9:00 PM."

"Okay, Sky!" Duane replied as Sky finished his meal and beer; off he went.

It was a warm Saturday night around nine when he decided to leave and asked Duane to see if Wally has a boarding room we can rent for the night so we can rest a bit so he did then went to find Sky at the Hospital too tell him. As he was coming out of the restaurant, just finished eating and had his last beer.

He walked out and started to walk across the street, and a car struck him and rolled him over the hood into the windshield and into the pavement as the car kept going, never stopping! Passers-by never saw the license plate or make of the car as police arrived to take a statement and the ambulance arrived to take Duane to Darwin General.

Sky was at the same hospital to check on O'Hara and POWs. He happened to look down the hall and saw Duane on a stretcher being wheeled into the operating room. No one was allowed in, and Sky was devastated. He wanted to know what happened. No one knew who hit Duane. He was lying there, unconcession!

In the meanwhile Sky checked on O'Hara, but he checked himself out and left. Sky went out to look for him as other POWs made their way back home the following day. Sky drove all over town, and every place he came to see if anyone had seen the general! Sky was showing everyone he met his picture he got from the president.

Sky got information on General Thomas O'Hara. He was trying to leave Australia! Trying to catch a flight back to the States. Sky found out where he was and went after him and found him at the airfield trying to board a passenger transport plane. He stopped him and told him, "You are my mission from the president!" And he was the only one to send him back to the States! So he got him back into the Jeep and headed to his plane to send him back to Washington.

Sky got help from some MPs to watch the general on the president's orders. He wanted to make a phone call to find out what had happened to Duane. Hospital staff couldn't tell him anything about his condition. So he needed to find out quickly because he was pressed for time! He went back to the C-46 and told the MPs to go, he would handle it from here! He grabbed the general by the throat and asked him what happened to Duane!

The general looked into Sky's eyes and said, "He is dead, like you're going to be!"

Sky replied, "What do you mean by that!"

The general replied, "You and Duane are in danger! And so am I if you don't get me back to the States!"

"By whom?" Sky replied.

"Dr. Sin!" the general replied. "Now get me out of here now! Get me back to the States immendaily!"

Sky had no choice but to head back home without his best friend, and he started the engines and got clearance to leave the airfield, and off he went back to the States, not knowing Duane's condition!

In the meanwhile, back in Darwin General Hospital, Duane was coming out of his coma. As he was waking up, things were coming in and out of focus as he was looking around the room. He noticed two men; they were MP's staring at him. They called him by rank. "Major McSwaine, Major McSwaine." They shook him.

Nurse Jenny walked in and asked the two, "What are you doing? Leave him alone, he's not quite well yet, he just came out of a coma. Please leave," she said angrily.

So the two men looked at each other and said to her that they were MP's and were investigating the murder of a salesman!

"A salesman?" Duane couldn't kill a salesman, he was here in a coma, she said.

"No, you don't understand, that's his code name, Salesman," said the MP's "He's working for us. He was on a case following a Nazi spy. We suspect one General Thomas O'Hara as a Nazis spy, but we can't prove it yet. We need Major McSwaine to give a statement saying that he suspects General O'Hara sabotaged the C-47 on their way to Australia. Lt. Col. Hawkins and the other GI must sign statements also. Now may we wake him, nurse."

"No, I don't care if you are the president himself now please leave before I call security and don't come back!"

"Oh, we'll be back with your government approval." And they left.

Duane wondered what the hell was going on.

Nurse Jenny said, "Don't worry, Duane. I've gotten rid of them for you."

"Who were they, and what did they want with me?"

Nurse Jenny explained as if she knew herself. "Something to do with being a Nazis spy named General something or other," she said.

"You mean General Thomas O'Hara."

"Yeah, that's him!"

"General Thomas O'Hara, they think I'm a spy also, and how about my best friend, Sky Hawkins, did they question him?"

"I don't know, but you're not safe here, those guys will be back."

While Duane was waiting for Jenny by the US Navy docks, he noticed his old friend that he and Sky knew. He called out to him. "Hey, Brooklyn!"

Lieutenant Commander Francis Terry Winslow looked back and noticed it was Duane! "How have you been? What happened to you! Were you in a battle or something!"

"No, nothing like that," he replied as they were shaking hands. "No, it's a long story," Duane replied.

"Hey, how's Sky doing? Is he with you?"

"No," Duane replied. "I am trying to get to Sydney! You know if there's a bus or truck going there!"

"No," Brooklyn replied. "My ship the USS MT *Vernon* (LSD-39) is heading for Midway. I just got off Liberty. Too bad, if I knew you were in town, I would look you up! Hey, Duane, Scuttle butt has it the MP's are looking for you and Sky. as Brooklyn spotted his Captain ready a board he asked for extension on his leave so spent time with Duane, captain and gave him another 48 hr. passes he said "thank you Skipper" as he saluted him and left with Duane The Captain wasn't aware events that about to unfolding at Midway Island he had orders stay in Brisbane until further orders!

As Duane said to Brooklyn "Yes, I know that is why I need to go to Sydney, get away from here, also I need to find a way back to the States, clear my name."

As he was turning to look for Jenny, he saw her walking across the street coming from the train depot, calling out his name and waving to Duane. He saw a car come barreling around the corner. It struck poor Sharon and killed her instantly.

Duane yelled at the top of his lungs, "Nooooooo! Jenny! Jenny!" As he ran to her aid, he cried, "Please, no! My god, no, not her please, get up, baby, please!"

The blood was all over the street. Brooklyn got a good look at the car. It was a 1941 Bentley Buick four-door with three passengers in it.

The license plate read K06714.

Duane was in tears, crying over the loss of his sweetheart Jenny. He couldn't believe his own eyes what just now happened!

Brooklyn tried to comfort him. "Duane," he said with a sad voice. "She's gone, I'm sorry, but nothing you can do for her now! Let's go to the police station, make a report. I have all the details, okay! Come on."

In the meantime, back in the States, a man approached the salon that Helen owned in Newark. He was looking for Helen Seamen. He walked up to the glass door and opened it as the bell rang to let them know customers were coming in.

Linda noticed the man and said, "Can I help you, sir!"

The man replied, "I'm looking for Helen! Helen Seamen, are you her?"

Linda laughed and said, "No, I'm not her! I'm just a friend, why do you want her for?" she asked, puzzled.

The man looked at Linda straight in the eyes, which sent chills to Linda's body. He answered, "Yes, you can, tell her Sky Hawkins is looking for her. Tell her to call me at this number, okay?"

Linda looked at the man strangely and said, "No, problem! Relay the messages there, anything else?" she asked.

The man shook his head no and left out the door.

Linda(who was filling in for Judy as she was getting ready for her night out with Sam, her new husband) was ready to call Helen when she just started to come in the door.

"I have a message for you, Helen," Linda replied, a little nervous. "About what just happened." And he handed her the note with the phone number on it and said, "Sky Hawkins wants you to call him as soon as possible, okay!" Meanwhile, Sky returned to Washington with the general as President Roosevelt requested, saluted the president and said to himself the mission accomplished. it been a whole year he been away on that mission It's now August 1942, He was thinking of Helen as he looked at the letter was waiting at oval office the president held for him when he return he gave the letter to Sky put it in his shirt pocket had in his shirt pull it out and he went outside to the nearest place to sit so he could read the letter he went on the White House lawn lean against a tree as he reading her letter he was thinking back to the summer of '41 before Pearl Harbor was attacked, when he spent his first summer with Helen. at the jersey shore It was a summer he never forgot! as he started to daydream about it.

City Maps for Neighboring States:
Delaware New York Pennsylvania

CHAPTER 9

The Jersey Shore

It was a warm summer evening around seven o'clock, and Sky stopped to get a bite to eat at the Blue Oyster Diner. He was tired and hungry after loading the C-46 Cargo Plane. He headed inside when he saw Helen there in the center of the dining room. He couldn't take his eyes off her as he made his way toward her. He put his hands covering her eyes and whispered in her right ear, "Guess who this is, Angel Face."

She jumped up with excitement and turned around and kissed him. "Sky!" she replied with a smile. "Where have you been, I miss you so much." And she hugged him, and Sky smiled as he pulled her chair back so she could sit back down. Sky sat next to her and just stared at her like she was the only woman in the room. The noise in the background faded away as she ordered her fish of filet. The band was playing her favorite song; she was humming to it as he got up from his chair, took her hand and smiled, and said to herself, "What a big handsome man he is," as Sky brushed her hair with his hand. They danced as Sky showed her the locket she gave him that night in Africa. She then smiled.

Sky looked up at his watch and noticed the time just flew by. And he looked into her eyes, gently touched her cheek, and kissed her as if it was their very last time. "I would love to see you again!" Sky replied with a smile.

As she blushed and smiled back and said, "Find with me! I'll be at the marina at six tomorrow night. I'm having a party for one of my best friends, Judy, she's getting married next Saturday. Come aboard if you like, it will be at pier 16 at seven o'clock tomorrow night."

Sky smiled and said, "I'll be there, baby!" Then he kissed her again as he put the money on the table and walked away out the door with his arm around her. As he walked her to her car and kissed her goodnight.

Sky went back to McGuire Army Air Corps Base to check on his cargo that he was sending to England Monday morning. He was leaving at six that morning.

As Helen went home to check on her mum, Kimberly Seamen, a lovely woman with dirty blonde hair like her daughter Helen. Helen kissed her mum as she left the parlor, reading her book. Helen told her mum all about Sky, this striking, handsome man with salt-and-pepper hair and with black mustache and hazel eyes. They talked for hours. She was getting tired and wanted to go to bed and dream of the man that stole her heart.

It was Saturday morning; Helen was planning a big party. Lots of friends and family would be there. She went shopping for a nice evening grown to impress her lover, Sky. Helen wanted to be on time for Judy's party, so she drove to the marina, got there at 6pm, Her friends and Cousins were starting to arrive, Her Mum kimberly Seaman, Judy's Mom Madeline and her father Jason Stills, her sister Georgina Stills, her Cousin Arelene, Cindy and Lucille, Brittany Landfield, Kathy Stanford, Caitlin Mcguire, Ruth Miller, Friends were Emily Maxwell, Jane Paine, Lynn Flowers, Debbie Beer and their boyfriends and husbands and of coarse her best friend the Guest of Honor Judy's Stills and her man Sam the man Reader, Sky called him. They all met at the pier heading toward her Cabin Cruiser, a Dark Brown wooden deck with brass rails and white bottom She was Helen's pride; she called her *Rosewood*; the name over the rose at the stern!

Everyone was there who she invited, except for Sky. He was held up at the airbase checking his manifest, making sure he had everything he ordered on board. It was getting to be 7:00 PM. Helen was wondering what was keeping Sky, the man who she remembered, the kiss and touch he left an impression on her that she couldn't forget.

It was now getting late, and Sky hadn't arrived yet. Everyone started to leave and said goodnight. It was about midnight. She was sad, disappointed because Sky hadn't shown up. She was finished locking up the cabin cruiser and starting to walk on the dock, and as she looked in a distance, a dark shadow of a man. She stopped and stared at the man from a distance where he was standing. He started walking toward her in the dark. Once he was underneath a streetlight, she recognized him. Sky! She cried out with tears running down her eyes. She ran to him and kissed him and hugged him and said, "You finally came!"

And she looked at him with hurt in her eyes and slapped him and said, "Why are you so late?"

He replied with a smile, "I had my cargo. I had to check on it, it took me longer than I thought. I'm sorry, honey." And he gave her a pink rose. He walked her to his Jeep, and they rode off into the night and found a motel where they spent the night.

The next morning, they woke up in each other's arms. They stopped for breakfast, and Sky drove her home and kissed her goodbye, and off he went heading to McGuire Army Corps Base to go to England. She never forgot the night they spent together. She would always keep that in her mind until they would meet again!

Helen was sad not hearing from Sky. She thought he would write to her from England, but days went by without a word, not even a phone call. She said to herself, "I must concentrate on my business." She was trying not to think about him as tears rolled down her face as she stared out the window at her beauty salon, watching people passing by.

Meanwhile in England, Sky landed on time at RAF Lake heath at 1:00 PM. There was an army truck waiting there to take the supplies he brought back from the US. He went into the hangar to talk to Staff Sergeant Smith(RAF) to get him a Jeep so he could go into town to get something to eat with Wing Commander Roy Storm Sutcliffe(RAF)(their old buddy Sky and Duane used to fly with him before the war! They hung out in London Town back then, Sky called him Stormin Norman because he comes in a place like a raging bull in a china shop he is 6ft. 9 in. solid all muscle now they back together once again).

As they both drove off toward Westminster, London to the Olde Towne Tavern Inn on Baker Street "I am going to give up the booze and one night stands, for her, I want to settle down in quiet little town with her Roy not like Elizabeth I went through hell with her she left me when I needed her the most Roy" As Sky's started to thinking about the different between Elizabeth and, Helen, he told Roy "Elizabeth just thought of herself and for Helen soft spoken and sweet and thoughtful that's my Helen, "Boy, what a gal", he said to Roy as he pulled out a handkerchief he had given her to wipe tears from her face when they said their goodbyes at Helen's door. He could still smell the perfume on the handkerchief that she wore last night that lingered in his mind as he drove out of the military base with Roy, Sky and had a smile on his face.

"I want to see her again, Roy when I return from England." Roy Replied "She sounds like my kinda gal!" Sky and Roy park in front of the pub went in order lunch and a ale they finished their lunch headed back to the base as London started getting bomb Roy asked Sky come down the air shelter Sky shook his head no because Sky was eager to go back to the States. He couldn't deal with war here in England; he had enough of the war and wanted to go back to the States where it was nice and peaceful. He went back to RAF Lakenheath to check his plane. It was undamaged, and he was relieved to see The C-46 was still in one piece. He shook Roy hand, said goodbye and got onboard, taxied out onto the runway, headed home. As he tilted his plane to the left, he could see London burning into the night. He said to himself, "What a terrible thing just happened to a town that was once so peaceful at one time." As he flew into the sunset heading home to a country, he was glad it wasn't scorned from this war.

As he headed across the sea, heading home he was looking forward to seeing Helen again.

Meanwhile, back in Newark, Helen headed home to see if there was a letter or a call from Sky. She came into the house, asked if her mum had any letter arrived or a phone call from him who she missed dearly, but nothing came, not even a phone call. She worried he might have forgotten her. It's been so long.

Sky arrived back to McGuire a few hours ago. He landed his plane and went inside to use the phone to call Helen, but she wasn't home. Helen took her mum grocery shopping. He hung up the phone and headed toward her house, hoping to see her when he arrived there.

She was helping her mother with groceries into the house, and as she turned to see who it was, she dropped the bag and ran to him with a big hug and a kiss. "I'm glad to see you. Why didn't you write or call me."

He said, "I'm sorry, there was a war going on, I lost track of time. I thought I could find the time. The army aircorps business keeps me going, I didn't have time to write. London's been bombed all through the day as I was leaving, damn Germans!" Sky yelled out in anger, and Helen calmed Sky down with a kiss.

"It's okay, baby," she said. "I'm glad you are back," she said as they walked into the house. "I'm glad you're safe and sound now. You are here. We can spend the night together. Let's go meet my mum."

"Hello, Mrs. Seaman, how are you?"

"I'm doing okay, I was sick for a while, thank God for Helen, I couldn't make it without her," she replied as Sky smiled.

"Your mum's a nice lady. I'm glad she's doing fine. Can we step outside, I'd like to talk to you about how I'm feeling about you."

She said, "Okay."

They went outside.

"I want to let you know how much I miss you and thought about you a while I was away, but I want you to come to Florida and live with me, Duane. I know you have a business here, but I'd like to take you home with me. And start a new life with me!"

"Sky! Are you proposing to me!" Helen was so thrilled.

"Yes, I am, but my job takes me all over the world. I might not have much time to spend with you! For it's my life, the army corps, but you live with me, I promise you I'll keep you happy and content. I always will love you no matter what, just stay with me, please, I can't live without you."

She said, "Let me think about it because of Mum and the salon. I too have too much to do here."

Sky said with a smile, "Okay, let's sleep on it and talk in the morning. We will take a ride to Wildwood. We will spend the weekend there!

She said, "Okay." She kissed him and smiled. "I'll see you tomorrow. I have to go back in to take care of Mum, but I'll call you tomorrow. Where are you staying?" she asked.

Sky answered, "I'm staying at the Shore Motel in Elizabeth. Call me there, I'll be waiting for your call!" He kissed her back and went to his Jeep and drove off as she stood by the door, smiling and waving goodbye.

It was Sunday morning. Sky woke up and decided to call her at 7:00 AM.

She answered and said, "I was about to call you, when are you coming over?"

"I'll pick you up around eight. Go have breakfast and then head to the beach."

"Okay, baby, I'll see you then. I love you, bye." Then she hung up, and got ready for their weekend date!

Eight o'clock rolled around, and Sky pulled up into her driveway. He jumped out of his Jeep and walked toward the door, rang the doorbell. She looked through the curtain. She could see it was Sky! With his sunglasses and Hawaiian shirt and white shorts. She was so excited to see him again. She had on a white sundress and a straw hat and sunglasses. She opened the door and kissed him as he was walking in. He turned to Helen's mum to greet her as Helen then kissed her mum goodbye, and off they went to Wildwood.

As they jumped on the New Jersey turnpike heading South, Sky and Helen joked with each other and were talking, and they both were laughing, kissing. He put his arm around her. They finally made it to the Jersey shore on Wildwood. You could see the ocean from a distance. It was beautiful.

They parked by a restaurant where they were going to have breakfast, in Horizon. Sky spotted it, something from a distance. He ran back to his Jeep to get his binoculars to see what was in the water.

Sure enough, he spotted a German U-boat about five miles offshore. Sky told Helen to go into the diner. "I'll be there soon," Sky said.

Sky went to his Jeep and used his two-way receiver to call the Authority of this sighting. Sky went into the diner and told Helen what he saw as they ordered breakfast. Helen was amazed about the sighting as their breakfast was being served.

"Are you kidding me?" she replied.

After they ate, they went outside toward the beach. They looked through the binoculars and saw the top of the conning tower of the U-boat. It was doing fifteen knots, just patrolling the Jersey Shore heading North.

By the time the police arrived, it was too late. The U-boat was gone. Cops took down Sky's statement and left. Sky and Helen were amazed at what they witnessed that close to shore! As they lay on the beach, they heard a scream from the water. It was very humid out, and as they both stood up, they saw what the problem might be. Looking at the water, they could see splashing and thrusting a Great White. It must have weighed a ton, a huge mother of a fish just ate a human whole. Blood was in the water as people panicked and screamed, and the lifeguard was yelling, "Get out of the water!"

Helen and Sky were stunned to witness this tragedy. They held each other in disbelief at what they saw. In minutes, the victim and shark are gone! Helen turned to Sky and cried on his shoulders while he was rubbing her back. He stared at the sea as it came back to normal, like nothing had happened. They both sat down on the white sand and looked at each other like this for real! Shark attack! On the Jersey Shores.

It was just too much for them, so they decided to take a walk on the beach, holding each other's hands, as they were once again in their own world. Walking toward the pier, they decided it was time to disappear to the other side of the beach, where there would be fewer people. They walked for miles on the shore. The sunset was so breathtaking as they watched it go down. Sky collected some driftwood and started a fire; they sat by the bomb fire, kissing.

They were enjoying each other's company when three men approached them. One of them made a nasty remark about his clothes. Sky yelled back at them as they were laughing, and that's when Sky jumped up quickly as he yelled at them as they headed down toward the water. Helen got scared and told Sky, "Don't bother with them, they look mean."

Sky told her it would be all right, got up, ran after them, and punched one of them in the face. The other one pulled a knife and stabbed Sky on the side as all three men ran off, leaving Sky bleeding in the sand. Helen helped Sky up onto his feet and started to walk up to a cottage nearby. She knocked on the door, crying for help. A couple answered the door and saw in shock a man and a woman, with Helen holding Sky up as blood was all over them. The couple helped Sky to the couch and lay him down as the woman got a pan of water to dress the wound and wrapped a bandage around it. Helen was grateful for them for saving the life of the man she loved so much.

An aerial picture showing the dramatic capture of German submarine U-571 during World War II (Henry Aldridge & Son)

Sky lay on the couch and put his hand on the bandage. He hoped he would be able to move, but the man told Sky it was a deep wound and may need stitches. "You must lay still, I'll call the ambulance, they'll be here soon enough, don't move."

Helen had tears coming down her face, and the woman comforted her, saying he will be alright! "My name is Jackie Freeman, and my husband's name is Ray Freeman, from Montreal. We come down here every summer and rent the same cottage!"

Helen looked up at her. "I'm Helen Seaman, and this is my fiancé, Sky Hawkins. We came down for the weekend to get away and that turned into a nightmare!" Helen was shaking as Jackie comforted her, saying, "He'll be alright, he'll be alright, don't worry. Ambulance will be here soon."

The ambulance came and took him away as Helen thanked them again, and Jackie and Ray waved goodbye as they closed the door.

They reach the hospital, and the doctor tells Helen, "I'll stitch him up. He'll be fine, so let him rest a bit. He'll be as good as new. You can take him home. I gave some painkillers. Take them as needed for the pain!"

"Thank you, Doctor," Helen replied.

Sky opened his eyes with a smile on his face and saw the woman he loved by his side. He grabbed her down so he could kiss her and smiled. "Helen, I love you, let's head back to your house."

Helen replied, "Yes, you can rest there, you can get your Jeep in the morning. Okay, honey, we will call a taxi, get back to the diner, get your Jeep, then we will head home, sweetie." She replied in joy that Sky was fine now.

It was July 4, 1941. Next Morning. Sky and Helen got his Jeep and headed home to Union City. Helen's mum Kimberly was just waking up from her chair as Helen and Sky arrived, Helen didn't want to worry her mum and said to her, "We had a little accident at the beach!"

Her mum said, "Okay, I'm going in the kitchen to make lunch for us!"

"Okay, Mum," Helen answered with a smile.

That was when Sky asked Helen to come back with him to Palm Beach FL where they could live and get married! She smiled and kissed him and said, "Okay, when are we going to leave?"

"Tomorrow, at one," he replied.

"Good, that gives me enough time to say my goodbyes to my coworkers. Have Judy take care of the salon for me while I'm away."

So next morning, after breakfast, she told her mum, "I'm going to Palm Beach FL to live with Sky, come along."

But her mum refused to leave New Jersey and said, "I'll be down for the winter months." She kissed them both and wished them well.

Then off to the salon to tell Judy, kiss her goodbye. Both looked at each other crying and hugging while Sky waited in the Jeep. Then Helen joined him, waving goodbye as they headed to McGuire Army Corps Base to head to Army Corps Base in Eglin, Florida.

Sky got the clearance for Helen to come on base, and they headed aboard the plane and headed South. They were airborne, and Helen was sitting on the copilot side and got a great view of the area, heading toward Maryland flew over Virginia then Carolina. She'd never flown before, and she loved the view from above, then Sky headed above the clouds. She looked down at them as if they were cotton. She was amazed at how it looked twenty thousand feet in the air.

Hours passed, and he reached the coast of Florida and landed in Eglin Air Corp Base and departed from C-46. They walked to the gate as military personnel were passing by as they made their way to the gate and got into his red Jag with Helen by his side. He was in his glory as they made their way home.

He found a note that said, "Hey, buddy, I'm headed to play golf with Dean. Hope to be back soon, Duane." Duane finally came home, said hi to Helen. and Said "boy you still look good since I last saw you in Cape of Good Hope". He couldn't believe what a beauty queen she was. He told Sky 'you hit the Jacket pot' to toast them with a glass of beer then said goodnight went to his room, went to sleep and left the two love birds alone.

It was now 3 years after last time they been to the Jersey Shore May 11, 1944 Helen 24 Birthday they started of the day boating then amusement park then a movie that evening alone in her Chris Craft the Rosewood having dinner Sky prepare her favorite dish filet of fish and toss salad by a candlelight and playing on the radio Moonlight Serenade it was a romantic evening after dinner they dancing until midnight on the deck under moonlight then Sky lift her up back to cabin kick the door shut and lay her in bed start kissing her Passionately both got undress and make passionate love with Besame Mucho was playing on the radio that morning Sky woke up first went out and surprise her with her favorite pink rose and a note on his pillow when she woke up few hours later found he was gone she sat up in bed grab the pink rose smelling it as she read the note it said my Darling angel face i have go on a mission to England but when I return I will marry you I love you forever until stars burn never more you make my life complete yours forever Sky as tears fell from her face she got up and got dress lock the cabin up and walk on deck towards her car thinking what a weekend it was best birthday, never! boating then a movie called Practically yours she said to herself, "My Romeo Sky" as she got into her car as she put on Sky sunglasses smiling as she put into first gear and drove off back home!

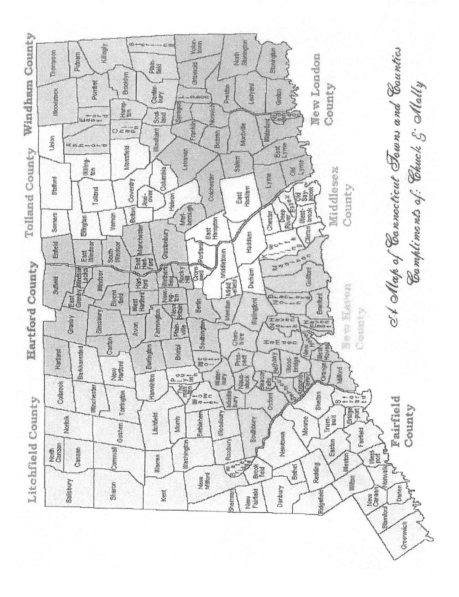

It's now June 6, 1944. A month after he was with Helen in the Jersey Shore, Sky and Duane were making a critical supply run at RAF Appledram Airfield England. That morning, as they unloaded his plane into another C-46, he decided to get some chow in the mess hall, As he was waiting in the chow line, he heard a voice behind him calling out. "Hey, Jimmy!"

He hadn't heard that since his childhood. His family and friends used to call him that a long time ago!

"Hey, Jimmy!" the voice called out again and again. "Hey, Jimmy!" As Sky was getting his chow.

Sky looked behind him, and sitting down next to him was his Cousin Jack Stern, whom he hadn't seen since they were kids.

"How the hell have you been, Scooter?" It was the nickname Sky gave him when they were kids because Jack loved building and riding motorbikes and racing them!

Both men shook hands. "Good, Jimmy, and you!"

"Great!" Sky replied.

"Wow! I haven't seen you in a dog's age."

Sky replied, laughing, "Yeah look at you, a lieutenant colonel."

"And you are a captain and in 82nd Airborne."

Both men were laughing with their arms around each other, still shaking hands, and in amazement, shaking their heads in disbelief. this my buddy and copilot Duane Mcswaine Duane met my cousin Jack Stern.

"Come sit right here with me and chat awhile."

So they did and talked about their childhood and laughed about the good old days in Chicago. Jack lived in Hyde Park, where they were Boy Scouts together, talking about who got the most merit badges they got as Boy Scouts, dating girls, exchanging dates, taking Uncle Ralph's pickup truck when they were thirteen, putting on a wooden block on the bottom of their right foot so they could reach the accelerators, Vinny Jones they both wonder how he was doing and where he is station nowThe men chatted as time went by, it seemed like yesterday as memories came alive once again in their eyes!

A lieutenant came over and tapped on Jack's right shoulder, telling him, "We're ready, sir!"

Both men got up, shaking hands again, and hugged each other goodbye!

"Nice to see you, Jimmy and nice meeting you Duane "the same here Jack" I wish you were flying the C-46 to our mission"

"No way Jack, both of us on the same mission it will be a disaster Jack" as they both start to laugh out loud "take care of yourself and happy landing, wherever you are flying to!"

"Same here, Scooter, keep in touch."

"Hey, hopefully, I'll be going home soon in Sunny California, San Diego, look me up sometime, Jimmy!"

Both men departed their separate ways waving goodbye. Sky watched as his cousin got ready aboard the C-46 with his parachute being put on and looking at each other as they nodded and shook their heads, waving and saluting each other with a smile as he boarded the C-46. The engines started roaring, getting ready to take off on the airfield, as the Sergeant was shutting the door for the D-day invasion.

Jack was one of the 82nd Airborne Division drop into France, and that day Jack got wounded in the leg and avoid capture with the help by the French Underground and rejoined his unit Eighty Deuce Airborne Division and held a strategic crossroads lead to Sainte Mere Eglise for rest invasion force to move in and take strong hold in France he was reward the purple heart for his outstanding bravery under heavy machine gun fire and He gets awarded The Legion of Honor by French Government by saving most of the division that day single handedly with M-60 Machine gun fully automatic onto the back of the Jeep he was in at the time!

And for Sky and Duane they headed back to the States, Sky wanted to be with the love of his life Helen and Duane wanted to play golf again. That would be the last time he would ever see his beloved cousin again!

CHAPTER 10

The SkyHawk Project

Two years had passed with no words about Duane's condition. Now he at Fort Edwards airforce base at the Cape in Mass design a new Jet F-16 turboJet first ever built anywhere Sky was head designer he knew what it will take so General O' Hara got the best officers he can find so he assign Sky head of the project sky agreed now as Sky called in Major Butch Stillwell 2nd Leiutenant Ken Stockton, Captain Mark Mainer, Colonel Mike Caliber (abserver from RCAF)Royal Canadian Air Force will it fly? No doubt, about it I'll stake my reputation on it," said Sky.

"That's good enough for me," replied The Colonel.

"That's easy for you to say, Colonel, I'll probably wind up flying the damn thing, of course!" said Captain Mainer as Major stillwell suggested he will fly the F16.

"Oh, no," said Sky. "I'm the one who designed it, and I'm the one to fly it!"

"Are you sure, Sky?" they asked.

"Yes, I'm sure, the general would kill me if I let any of his best fliers go before me!"

Sky's secretary, Ms. Camolott, entered the room and said, "Excuse me, but you have an urgent message on line one."

"Who is it?" asked Sky.

"I don't know, but he sounded quite upset."

"It must be General O'Hara calling to thank me for saving his life again," said Sky. "Excuse me, gentlemen" for a minute while I take this call." As they looked over the blueprints they looked at the Lieutenant as he said "amazing turbocharged engine the wave of the future the Soviets love gets hold of this!" as he shook his head.

Sky picked up the phone, and a voice said, "Is this Sky Hawkins?"

"May I ask who this is?" said Sky.

"Cut the baloney, you know damn well who this is!"

"Oh, General O'Hara!"

As his face turned red with anger, Sky knew the general's voice was timorous, but he knew he had no choice but to play along with the general's stupid game.

"Okay, General, what will it cost me to take this job?"

"Oh, first of all, you're not only going to design the latest planes but also be the test pilot too."

"Okay," Sky replied.

"Wait, that's not all, mister, you are also going to give me respect and full cooperation in anything I say. Understand, mister?"

"Yes, sir, I understand," Sky said. Knowing he was at the general's mercy.

"Now, first of all, you have to get a physical A good strong man like yourself should pass very easily."

"But I don't need a physical, I had one in 1931, that's good enough!" Sky said.

"No, it's not, good enough go get another one now, mister! Or I'm not going to assign you to fly your project. I will scrap the project!"

"Okay, okay," Sky replied. "I'll get another physical."

"Go see Doctor Roberts in the medical building across from hangar 9, and then report back to me."

"Yes, sir, is that all, sir?" Sky sarcastically replied.

"Don't get smart, do as you're told, mister, now move out!"

Sky got off the phone then he went back to the designing room and told all his officers he must get a physical. They saluted him and wished him good luck. Then he asked the staff sergeant at the desk, "Where about Hangar 9, I have to find the medical building?"

"Oh, okay, two barracks down, make a left, then a right, and it should be your second building on the right."

"Thank you, sergeant," Sky said.

"No problem, sir, anytime."

And off Sky went to get a physical.

When Sky arrived at the medical building, the doctor was waiting for him in the examining room.

"Yes, may I help you, young man?" asked the doctor.

"Yes, I'm here for a physical, General Thomas O'Hara sent me."

"Oh, you must be Lt. Col Hawkins! Sit on this table and take off your jacket and shirt."

Sky took off his jacket and shirt and asked, "Where can I hang these?"

"Right over there, behind the door," the doctor said.

The doctor proceeded with the examination, taking out a stethoscope, and asking Sky to breathe in and out as hard as possible. The doctor could hear a wheezing noise coming from Sky.

"What's that, Doc?" Sky asked.

"I don't know yet," said the doctor. "Do you smoke?"

"Of course not, I gave it up years ago," said Sky.

"Let me see your throat, open wide."

Sky complied with the doctor's request.

"Have you been in contact with pneumonia?" the doctor asked.

"Not since I was a kid, and they said I was cured."

"Well, I have to run some more tests before I can release you for work. I think it might be croup."

"What, are you nuts?" said Sky. "Where the hell would I get it from?"

"When you had pneumonia, when you were small."

"I've heard enough, let me out of here! Doc, please release me, I'll take my chances, okay?"

"Well, if your assignment means that much to you, all right, but I'm warning you to be careful in what you do from now on and take these pills I'm going to prescribe for you every four hours."

Then the doctor signed the release papers.

O'Hara called the good doctor to find out about Sky's condition, and the good doctor said he was fit to fly! Sky got back on the phone with the general and said "you got the Pentagon on the other line?"

Messerschmitt Me 323 - Wikipedia
en.wikipedia.org

Messerschmitt Me 323 Gigant (Giant) Six ...
militaryfactory.com

Transport, Messerschmitt Me-323 Gigant ...
flightsim.com

Messerschmitt Me 323 Gigant | Military ...
pinterest.com

Messerschmitt Me 323 Gigant Technical...
scale-model-aircraft.com

Messerschmitt Me 323 - Wikiped...
en.wikipedia.org

Messerschmitt Me 323 Gigant - ...
youtube.com

Messerschmitt Me 323 Gigant ...
thevintagenews.com

Messerschmitt Me 323 Gigant | ...
germanwarmachine.com

Messerschmitt Me 323 "Giant Sto...
alamy.com

Related searches

me-321

me 323 wreck

lego me 323

The Messerschmitt 323 Gigant in 26 P...
warhistoryonline.com

323 Gigant ("Giant") - German military ...
reddit.com

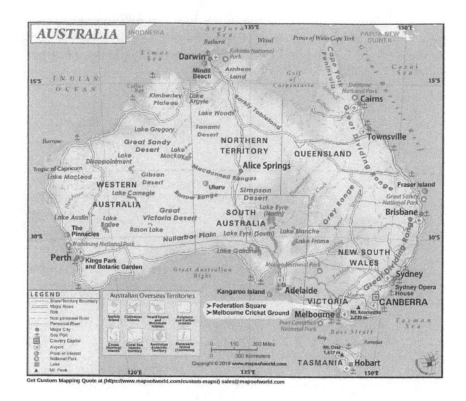

"That's right, Hawkins, I've got the Pentagon on the line here! Are you through with your little project yet?"

"It's only been a whole year that you started."

"Yes, but there are still bugs in it!" said Sky.

"I'm talking it over with your officers right now."

"You make sure those guys don't fly it!"

"Okay, okay, don't have a bird over it, sir!"

"I told them, I made it, and I'll fly it. It will be ready in a week, okay!" said Sky.

The general hung up without saying goodbye. Sky knew he had pushed his luck getting the plane ready on time, not knowing for sure what was really wrong with the design.

He knew he had not only the general on his back but also the Pentagon. "Politicians," he said. "I hate them more than the generals." Then he called his friends back into the room. "What do you think, gentlemen?"

Captain Mainer spoke first of the fuselage going behold the turbo charge at take off!" as they all start thinking what flight pattern he should take.

North by Northeast "Well, it's time to make this baby airborne," said Sky.

As the others shook his hand, they wished him well, and a Merry Christmas. And he thanked them for all their support, thinking that he wished Duane McSwaine was there to help him figure out the remaining problems. As he sat rubbing his face and back of his neck back and forth, saying to himself, "Those Machiavellians in Washington. If they only knew the massive amount of pressure they threw at me! Well, no sense thinking about it, I'm already elusive over it, and it's time to go home."

He locked his office door and noticed his secretary had already left, not aware he had let her go earlier. He walked toward the door, looking for his leather jacket, and smiled at Helen's picture, thinking he would see her at Christmas.

Washington wanted the schedule moved up, and Sky called Helen to see if she could attend the ceremony of the first flight of the turbojet *SkyHawk*.

"I would be delighted," said Helen. Sky told her his friends, the president, some congressmen, and of course, General Thomas O'Hara would attend. They spent the last night together at The Seabreeze Hotel. The beautiful view from Dennisport sunset was breathtaking as they watched it from the balcony on 5th fl. as they held each other and brushed her hair with his finger and turned to her and said "Baby we need this night together I love you forever "and smiled and turned her cheeks with his right hand and kissed her not far from the base that was the last time they ever were together.

The date was December 21, 1948. A typical New England winter day, wind speed of fifteen to twenty miles per hour, temperature about forty degrees, a possibility of some snow with a light frost on the wings of the jet. Sky walked from Hangar 9 as the crowd cheered him on. He waved and smiled back. Helen ran to him and kissed him good luck. With tears falling from her eyes, they hugged as if it was their last time.

Sky adjusted his helmet and climbed into the cockpit of the *Sky Hawk*. He proceeded to throw the switches and fire up the engines. As he taxied to the end of the runway, he waited for clearance from the tower.

The radio cracked with the voice of the controller. "Flight Sky Hawk, use runway six-four."

The plane roared down the runway, and the landing gear jumped from the ground and the plane, shooting into the winter sky, never to be seen again.

They searched for days, and only found fragments of the plane in Stonington on Deer Isle off the coast of Maine. Sky was never found.

CHAPTER 11

The Kidnapping of Helen Seaman

"A man stopped by earlier looking for you and said his name is Sky Hawkins. He looked at me kind of strange. Here's his number. He said for you to call him. He sent chills up and down my spine, and I asked him if there was anything else, and then he shook his head no and left. Is that weird or what?" asked Linda(who filling in for Judy)

Helen asked, "What did he look like? Did he have a mustache? Was his hair grayish? Did he have hazel eyes?"

"I think so. I'm not too sure! I was typing and filing. I really don't notice. But one thing I know is that he did have a deep sexy voice. Does that help you out, Helen?"

"Maybe, but thanks anyhow. Good night!"

"Good night, Helen. Have a nice weekend, see you Monday!"

"Oh, okay, thanks." And then she left wondering if that was Sky or if that was somebody else as she got into her car and went straight home.

The following day, she was awakened by a phone call. *Ring, ring, ring, ring.* Then she picked up the receiver. "Hello, who is this?" she asked.

"This is Sky Hawkins!" the man replied.

Helen got pretty upset and said, "Do you realize what time it is? I had to work late last night, and I am tired, so please hang up and don't call back!"

And the man hung up. Helen could not fall back to sleep. She got up, took her shower, ate breakfast, straightened the house a little bit, and went out. As she was getting into her car, a man across the street was watching her as she drove away. The man got into his car with another man driving and followed Helen down the road. She stopped at a red light, and that was when the two men got out of their cars and grabbed her out of her car.

She started screaming, "Leave me alone! Let me go!" She started kicking them and she struggled to get loose. That's when she kicked one of them right between the legs.

He went down on his knees yelling "Ah, ah, ah!" As she was running away from them, "Don't let her get away!" the man said as he was trying to get back up.

Helen was yelling, "Help me! Anybody, help me!" Of course, everyone stopped and stared as if she was nuts or something. As she was running around the corner, she smacked into Dr. Won Con Sin! (The one that got away from Sky Hawkins years earlier in Peru and killed his two friends, Dr. Leon Le Clerc and Dr. Thomas Cook.)

"Yes, young lady," he said as he was grabbing her by her wrist and held it up high. "May I help you?" he asked with his eerie laugh! "Ha, ha, ha, hi."

The two other men came racing around the corner and stopped dead in their tracks and said, "Good, you got her, Dr. Sin!"

"Yes! You fools you let her get away." And he pulled out his gun and shot them both dead. He started laughing again and again. Helen was scared and did not know what was going on, and she started crying. Poor Helen, she was shaking like a leaf, saying, "What do you want with me! I didn't do anything to you! Let me go at once!"

Dr. Sin looked at her and said, "You're Lover have forty-eight hours to show up at this address, 22 Cleafville Road, and drop off what he stole from me, or else you can kiss your pretty head goodbye."

She asked, "How is he supposed to know what's going on?"

"Oh, don't you worry, gorgeous. General O'Hara left a note in Sky Hawkins's office at Fort Edwards Air Force Base in Massachusetts."

Helen replied, "But that won't be long enough for him to reply!"

"It better be, for your sake."

Then he told his henchmen to drive off. Sin said, "My dear, maybe we'll take a trip to my country estate. Have you ever been to China? Did you ever see the Qinling Shan mountain range in northern China? It extends across Gansu, Shaanxi, and Henan province. The highest peak is 13,500 feet. Qin-huang-dao, the seaport in northeast Hebei province northeast of China, population 1,144,000, and Qinghai northwest of China northeast of Tibet."

As if Helen was really interested in listening to this.

"Yes, maybe we'll take a trip instead and let Sky Hawkins fight me in my territory for a change." Dr. Sin spoke Chinese to his driver and told him to go to an airport because they were going to China.

Then Helen said with anger on her face, "Wherever you take me, Sky Hawkins will track you down, and I'll watch him kill you!" She started staring out the window as they headed toward an airport. "I don't think so he has troubles of his own! Sin told Helen as she turned to look at him "What! did do to him what" said nervously frighent for Sky safety "you will know in do time you will know" Dr. sin gridding looking at Helen.

CHAPTER 12

A Farewell Salute To L.t. Col. James Micheal Stern

October 18, 1948. It has been 10 months since Sky Hawkins had gone missing over the coast of Maine, in Stonington, which is located on Deer Isle.(a month to the day after their 2nd wedding anniversary passed by Sky and Helen didn't celebrate it together)

It had been three hours since the kidnapping of Helen Seamen. Helen was sitting in the backseat on the other side, the car door open and dark hair land came in and didn't say a word and Helen looked at her and asked "why are you looking at me that way and what do you want from me?" as the dark hair lady just squinting not saying a word and poor Helen shaking with tears in her eyes coming down she was wiping the tears away as she turned her head looking out the window thinking of Sky. Meanwhile back in Brisbane as For Duane Elton McSwaine, with their good friend in Brisbane, Francis T. Winslow, the lieutenant commander of LSD-39 MT *Vernon*.

They had a lead to a 1944 black Bentley registered to one General Thomas O'Hara, who right now was meeting with Dr. Won Con Sin in Singapore with Helen in the backseat with the dark hair Mysterious women.

Duane and Brooklyn took a train to Sydney (with tickets Sharon bought when she got killed) they were all boarding a flight to Singapore from Sydney, Australia, that would depart in fifteen minutes. Duane couldn't wait to get his hands on General O'Hara.

He has waited a long time for this. "Now it's time for him to die!" Duane said to himself.

The MPs were still looking for Duane. They found out what happened to Sharon, and Helen learned that General O'Hara was working for Dr. Sin now! They notified the British authority of what had been going on and asked them to hold Major Duane Elton McSwaine and L.t. Comm. Francis Terry Winslow until the US government came to get them. The British authority agreed.

In the meanwhile, thirteen hours had passed since Helen and dark hair lady Dr. Sin and his henchmen Wong Ping arrived in Singapore. As they were departing, they noticed the police were everywhere. They did not want to take any chance that Helen would say something, so he ordered Wong Ping to get the car parked next to the terminal. He did, and then they drove off without being seen.

Forty-five minutes later, Duane and Brooklyn landed in Singapore, but the police were waiting for them. Brooklyn said, "Hey, Duane, look at the cops all over the airport, what do you think they want?"

"I don't know, but what Sky always says, I'm not sticking around to find out, so let's get out of here." And so they blended in with crowds coming out of the plane and exited from the nearest door out of the airport.

Dr. Sin met General O'Hara at his remote temple on BoHai Shandong peninsula off the Yellow Sea, and poor Helen was strapped to a table in the temple about to be sacrificed to Buddha. About twenty hours had passed, and now Sky Hawkins had twenty-eight hours left to find her.

General O'Hara came to the temple where Helen was and told her, "Your boyfriend, Sky Hawkins, died in a plane crash somewhere in Maine."

"No! No!" she said. "He's not dead! You want me to believe that!" And she started crying.

Dr. Sin said, "You fool! Why did you kill him, I need the Gold Crucifix which he stole from me in Peru!"

"Don't worry, Dr. Sin, don't worry, I have someone looking for it."

"We'd believe that Johnny has it if we lure Johnny here for the trade, he will agree to give us The Gold Crucifix." for her life.

And they both left the room laughing while leaving poor Helen to be sacrificed in less than twenty-eight hours.

Meanwhile in Maine, Sky Hawkins was found by a lobster boat crew, washed up on the shore of an island, and they found him. He was very pale and weighed about 160 pounds with a dislocated shoulder and a thick scraggly beard. He had lived on whatever he could find on the island.

Sky found himself in another hospital, this time in Bangor, with a dislocated shoulder. FBI agents were waiting for him to recover.

"What the hell is going on here?" Sky asked in anger.

One agent replied, "Calm down, Sky, calm down."

"We have information that might get you even more upset."

"What? What is it?"

"Do you know women named Helen Seamen?"

"Yes! Yes, I do, why? What's wrong?" Sky asked worriedly.

"Well, we're afraid she has been kidnapped by General O'Hara and Dr. Won Con Sin. We found this note saying you have forty-eight hours to give up the Gold Crucifix, which we found out is priceless, and then the note also said to bring it alone, with no tricks, to Singapore, at a shipyard where you'll get more instructions about what to do next."

"When did you find this note?" Sky asked in fractious, not believing what was happening.

"About ten hours ago," one FBI agent replied.

"I've got less than thirty hours to save her! You guys have to get me out of here and set me up with weights and a ninja instructor to train me! Dr. Sin has no mercy on his victims when it comes to martial arts!" Sky replied.

"No problem, we'll get you released as soon as possible and set you up at Fort Drum in Watertown, New York, for your training. You'll get our full cooperation."

Then within five hours, Sky found himself up at Fort Drum, training and lifting weights. Within less than ten hours left to save

Helen, he flew to Singapore with the Gold Crucifix that the FBI gave him from a museum in Washington, DC.

Sky flew in a Douglas F3D(F10) Skyknight, he called the *Cobra*. He arrived in Singapore less than an hour—half the time it would have taken in the *Phantom*. As he made his way through a British Air Force base, he wasted no time in getting to the shipyard. He looked at his watch; it was now 8:45 PM. He had just about two hours to spare.

A short Chinese man walked to him and asked him, "Are you the one they call Sky Hawkins?"

Sky turned around and grabbed the short Chinese man by the throat and whaled him into the wall and said, "Yes, why do you ask?"

The man started choking and said, "Let me go, I can't breathe!"

"Where's Con Sin? Tell me now, or I'll kill you hard."

"I'll take you to him!"

"No tricks, or you're dead. You got that Chinaman?"

"Yes, no tricks!"

And they got into a car and drove off.

In the meantime, they were being tailed, and so Sky said, "Lose them!"

They tried but couldn't shake the car that was following them. Then Sky told him to pull a sharp turn in the middle of the street, and so he did, stopping right in the middle and blocking the car so they could not go around them. The car stopped dead, and the bumper came dozens of hitting Sky as he got out of the car. Sky pulled out his .45 pistol and said, "Whoever is in there, get out very slowly, where I can see you!"

And so they did.

"Duane, is that you?"

"Yes! It's me, Sky, yeah it's me! Boy, you have grown a beard!"

"What the hell are you doing here?"

"You remember Brooklyn?"

"Oh yes," Sky replied. "Long time no see." And they shook hands. "Are you still living in New York City?"

"Oh, of course, I wouldn't live anywhere else in the world! Can't wait to get back after Midway to Pearl then San Diego and flight home to New York, I got an extension on my Liberty so I won't be AWOL!" (absent without leave)!"

As the three men were talking, a pretty Black Woman came screaming out of the tavern across the street.

"Help! Help! Anybody, they're going to kill my boyfriend!"

Sky, Duane, and Brooklyn ran across the street to help the young lady.

"May we be of some assistance to you, ma'am?" Sky asked.

"Yes, please, they're going to kill my boyfriend! Help him, please!"

And so they all ran in, and Sky shot a couple of rounds in the air to get their attention. They all turned around and looked at Sky, Duane, and Brooklyn. At that moment, Duane turned to Sky and said, "This isn't the time or the place to be a hero. We're outnumbered ten to three!"

Sky looked at Duane, smiled and winked his eye.

"Oh no! Here we go again." Duane replied frantically.

Francis looked at both of them and said, "What! What is going to happen?"

Sky told Duane and Brooklyn to watch his back. As Sky cautiously walked to, thugs were holding down three Tuskegee AirCorps Pilots Their names were Vinney Jones, Alex Powers, and Arthur Miles. Sky Recognized it was Vinny, He knew him since back in 1925 in Chicago he was his best friend. "Hey! I advise you guys to get off them!" he told them in anger!"

"Oh yeah, says who?" "What are you going to do about it?" one huge mean Australian guy said to Sky.

As he pulled out a huge knife, a huge man said "what are you going to do about it big mouth!" Sky looked the huge man straight in the eyes and then shrugged his shoulders and turned around and that's when the huge man said, "That's what I thought you would do!"

Sky turned with his right foot high in the air and kicked him from his left cheek to right cheek and then kicked 'em hard as he could in his upper chest and watched him fly over some tables and chairs, and he knocked the huge man out cold.

Then he asked, "Who's next in line?" And the rest of them took off, running scared.

He helped his childhood friends up, and all six men went out the door, and Vinney's fiancée ran to him and hugged him and asked if he was all right.

And he said, "Yeah thanks to an old buddy." They all shook hands, and Vinney said, "This is my fiancée Mary! Mary, this is Sky." and when Sky introduced Duane and Brooklyn, Sky and Vinny shook hands then they hugged Vinny and replied "I miss you old buddy!" Sky replied "Same here Vinny been too long I wish you the best with your fiance keep in touch" then he kissed Mary on the cheeks and waved goodbye because he knew he was pressing for time!

That's when Sky noticed the Chinaman had left and told his other two friends Brooklyn and Duane, "Come on, we must find him, I've got less than an hour to find Helen." Sky and Duane got in Sky's jeep to look for the Chinaman.

The Chinaman got a hold of Dr. Won Con Sin and told him, "The man they call Sky is alive and looking for you."

"He's alive Good! Where is he?"

"He's coming this way, and I'll lead him to you, and he has his friends with him too!" the Chinaman replied.

"That's okay. Let them all come. The more, the merrier." And he started laughing. "Ha! Ha! Ha!" And they both hung up.

Brooklyn noticed the Chinaman first. "Hey, guys, there's the Chinaman he wants us to follow. He is waving us on!"

"So follow him, we have no choice," Sky replied.

And as they did, they crossed one bridge. As soon as they got across, the Chinaman pulled over and blew it up.

Duane said, "There's no turning back now!"

"You got that right!" Brooklyn replied.

Then they watched the car pull a hole shot and drove like a bat out of hell.

"Follow him! Don't lose him!" Brooklyn replied eagerly.

Off they went chasing the Chinaman up a narrow mountainside until they found the temple. The Chinaman got out of his car and ran into the temple with Sky, Duane, and Brooklyn not far behind him. As soon as they got through the temple doors, they stopped and looked around, and an eerie voice called out! "Sky! Sky Hawkins, do you have the Gold Crucifix?"

The Gold Crucifix. Weighing in at 20K, it stood three feet tall. Made during the fourteenth century by the Spanish settlers and brought as a gift to the Quechua Indians, it was priceless. Hitler heard it held God's Powers and anyone process it has God's powers and Sin thought if he gave it Hitler, he could conquer the world with God on his side! As history prevailed The Nazis were defeated and Duane returned the Crucifix to The Quechua Indians, and in return, they gave Duane Spanish gold coins that were worth millions in a chest. And Duane shared it with Helen.

"Yes, I do. Where the hell on earth are you, Won Con Sin?"

And the voice answered, "You! And you alone, step up these stairs and come into my house of worship!"

Sky did not waste any time, hopping up the sparrow staircase. As soon as he was at the top, he opened the thick wooden doors that led inside and saw Helen on a table in front of the huge Buddha. He said to Hellen, "I'm here, angel face! I'll cut you loose!"

As soon as he said that, Con Sin jumped him from behind and threw him against the temple walls. Saying, "I'm here, angel face, to save you! Who is going to save you! You fool!" As he finished saying that, he thought Sky was now unconscious and walked up to him with his Samurai sword, ready to strike him dead! Sky swung around to his right side and shot him twice in the head, and Dr. Won Con Sin looked at him and laughed and dropped on top of Sky Hawkins.

Then Sky pushed him off then started cutting the ropes that held Helen to the table when all of a sudden two more people came walking into the room. It was General O'Hara and Elizabeth Grenchmen!(the dark hair women who sat beside Helen in the back-seat) And coming up from behind them were Duane McSwaine and Brooklyn.

Duane jumped the general from behind and said, "This is for Jenny!" As he slit his throat wide open. He dropped to the floor in his pool of blood.

Elizabeth reached in her Jacket, pulled out a revolver, looked at Sky, and said, "You made my life miserable, and now it's your turn." Then she pointed the gun at Helen and shot it! Sky leaped in front of Helen as he was saying, "Nooooo!"

He took the bullet in the chest, turned, and said, "My life for you," and collapsed into her arms.

Helen grabbed the .45 out of Sky's holster while Sky was still in her arms and shot Elizabeth.

She fell dead to the floor.

She held him in her arms with tears falling from her eyes. Sky looked up at her, reached out, with his dying breath and reach up to kissed her for the very last time. As he did she told him "Remember our last night together you got me pregnant finally I am going to have your child she or he will always remind me of you" and the times we had together I Will let our child know all about you your legacy will lived on in our kid always and I wearing the gold cross your mom left you that you gave to me I never ever taking off I Always love you sweetheart". He smiled as he collapsed in her arms once again and with his last breath and choking and gasping for air blood filling his lungs and running out on the side of his mouth and said " I going to the spirit in the sky" look at her with tears falling from side of his face collapse into her arms as she looked at his lifeless body and sobbing and then kiss him on the lips and said her goodbyes and then she gave out aloud "scream and said nooooo! You can't be gone!" We are supposed to have a good married life together and now you're gone. She looked into his palm as the locket she gave him in Africa the night they met and she closed his hand and cried even harder with her head touching him. Then She closed his eyes and kissed him for the very last time then started to cry Hysterically as Brooklyn and Duane tried to comfort her as they pick up Sky and carry him back to his jeep with Helen holding him and made their way back to the states where he once love Palm Beach Fl. and had a burial at sea the military had a 21 gun salute and a C-46 flew over the watery grave for a dead warrior Sky Hawkin. his close friends Mario, Cliff, Dave, Eric, Joe and Al, their sister Carmella Pasquale and Derek, they worn a suit and tie, Duane, Dean, and Brooklyn, Jack, Roy(RAF), Mike(RCAF)Vinny, Dustin, Nick in their class-A saluted the C-46 as it flew over the burial site after they toss his ashes to the sea and Duane said "We will always remember a man who touch our lives Lt. Col. James Michael Stern (Sky Hawkins) as he flies above the clouds once again we salute you! Helen cried as the air force staff sergeant handed to her the folded flag as (PFC) blew taps. Helen requested.

James looked up with tears in his eyes as a voice called out to him.

"Why are you reading Grandma's diary?"

"I thought it was yours, Dad!"

"That was before my time."

Then he closed it and gave it to James Michael Stem Sr.

"How did Grandpa get that name anyhow, Dad?" "Does Gram still have the Gold cross?

"Grandpa got that name from his friends in the army aircorps because he was a hotshot pilot in his time."" yes Grandma Stern still wears the Gold Cross till this day she never take it off"

Then James smiled and said, "Dad, I'm going to be like him. Someday I want to be like Grandpa a hot shot pilot"

"Sure, son, sure."

Then they both smiled as they closed the lights and closed the door and went down the stairs.

The End

The Adventures of Sky Hawkins
and Duane McSwaine

Also in March of 1943, Sky Hawkins and Duane McSwaine made some daring supply drops behind enemy lines, to their Russian comrades at Leningrad, Minsk, Kyiv, Kharkiv, and also Rostov.

They picked up the supplies at Stockholm, Sweden, flew to Leningrad overnight, and started the airdrops to the Russian front lines. It lasted for eight weeks, flying back and forth through rain, snowstorms, and sleet; these didn't stop them until Germans bombarded them with too much flak. It was too much for the mighty *Phantom*, the C-46, to handle, so that's when they decided to scrub the mission. Altogether, they spent 448 hours flying.

That's when they also decided to head for Moscow for some rest and relaxation. And have the *Phantom* checked for minor damage. When they landed in Moscow in March of 1943, they were overwhelmed by the reception from their Russian comrades, cheering them on and lifting them both way up high on their shoulders. They paraded them around like they won the war singlehandedly on the airfield. Finally, they let them down in front of their aircraft. And that's when they got their picture taken together; that would be their last picture ever! Talking together, arm in arm, with their thumbs up, duane wearing his favorite red baseball cap he always wore and Sky wore his officer cap wearing their pilot sunglasses and smiling in front of the camera. Then they waved back at the crowds; it was a proud moment for the boys.(Duane kept that photo in his flight Jacket for (remembrance of his falling servicemen and best friend Sky

Hawkins) The Russians loved them for what they had done for them they got The Order of Victory from Joseph Stalin leader of Soviet Union.

Duane had a picture Hellen and Sky when they first met, made into a painting when they were in Soweto in S.A. for Helen and Sky for a wedding gift. Helen Seamen and Sky Hawkins secretly wed on June 18, 1945.in NewBurgh, N.Y. at Lord Grace chapel and honeymoon up Lake George N.Y. No one knew about this wedding except, of course, Duane, the best man, and Georgina Stills, she was the maid of honor and Helen best friend Judy and her husband Sam the man Reader also was there last time Sky and Hellen were together in the Cape last romancing weekend before he disappearance she got pregnant A nine months later, September 2, 1949, Georgina and Duane became proud godparents of James Michael Jr. Duane made that picture of him and Sky when they were in the Soviet Union in 1943 into a painting also given to James Jr. On his wedding day, June 30 James got it hung in his den as a reminder of good friends that were through the time when America was in turmoil!

Sky never got the chance to meet the boy he wanted so much!